PENGUIN CLASSICS

A Maigret Christmas

'Extraordinary masterpieces

'A brilliant writer'

– India Knight

'Intense atmosphere and resonant detail . . . make Simenon's fiction remarkably like life'

– Julian Barnes

'A truly wonderful writer . . . marvellously readable – lucid, simple, absolutely in tune with the world he creates'

– Muriel Spark

'Few writers have ever conveyed with such a sure touch, the bleakness of human life'

– A. N. Wilson

'Compelling, remorseless, brilliant'

– John Gray

'A writer of genius, one whose simplicity of language creates indelible images that the florid stylists of our own day can only dream of'

– *Daily Mail*

'The mysteries of the human personality are revealed in all their disconcerting complexity'

– Anita Brookner

'One of the greatest writers of our time' – *The Sunday Times*

'I love reading Simenon. He makes me think of Chekhov'

– William Faulkner

'One of the great psychological novelists of this century'

– *Independent*

'The greatest of all, the most genuine novelist we have had in literature'

– André Gide

'Simenon ought to be spoken of in the same breath as Camus, Beckett and Kafka' – *Independent on Sunday*

GEORGES SIMENON

A Maigret Christmas

Translated by DAVID COWARD

PENGUIN BOOKS

PENGUIN CLASSICS

UK | USA | Canada | Ireland | Australia
India | New Zealand | South Africa

Penguin Books is part of the Penguin Random House group of companies
whose addresses can be found at global.penguinrandomhouse.com.

Penguin
Random House
UK

First published in French as *Un Noël de Maigret* by Presses de le Cité, 1951
This translation first published 2017
This edition published 2018

008

Set in 12.5/15 pt Dante MT Std
Typeset by Jouve (UK), Milton Keynes
Printed and bound in Great Britain by Clays Ltd, Elcograf S.p.A.

ISBN: 978–0–241–35674–6

www.greenpenguin.co.uk

MIX
Paper from
responsible sources
FSC® C018179

Penguin Random House is committed to a
sustainable future for our business, our readers
and our planet. This book is made from Forest
Stewardship Council® certified paper.

Contents

A Maigret Christmas

1.

It was always the same, every time. As he settled down in bed, he had sighed, as usual:

'Tomorrow, I shall sleep in.'

And Madame Maigret had taken him at his word, as though the years had taught her nothing, as if she had not learned to attach no importance whatsoever to sentiments uttered in this way. She could have slept in too. There was no reason why she should get up early.

But it was not yet first light when he heard her carefully stirring between the sheets. He had not budged. He had forced himself to breathe regularly and deeply, like a man fast asleep. It was almost a game. He was touched when he felt her working her way to the edge of the bed as cautiously as an animal, and stopping after each movement to check that he had not woken up. There came the moment he always waited for, in a state almost of suspense, when the bedsprings, relieved of his wife's weight, would relax with a sound like a sigh.

She gathered her clothes from the chair, took for ever turning the knob of the bathroom door and eventually, far away in the kitchen, allowed herself to move about normally.

He had gone back to sleep. Not deeply and not for very long, though long enough to have a confused, rather maudlin dream. Later, he would remember nothing about it but he knew it had been sad and it had left him in a state of heightened sensitivity.

A long stripe of pale light was visible between the curtains, which never closed fully. He lay there a little longer, on his back, with his eyes open. The aroma of coffee came to him, and when he heard the front door of the apartment open and close, he knew that Madame Maigret had rushed down the stairs and gone out to buy him warm croissants.

He never ate anything in the morning, making do with black coffee. But this was another ritual, one of his wife's ideas. On Sundays and public holidays, he was supposed to stay in bed until late morning, and she would pop out and get croissants for him from the shop on the corner of Rue Amelot.

He got out of bed, slid his feet into his slippers, put on his dressing gown and opened the curtains. He knew he was in the wrong and that she'd be upset. He would have done anything to keep her happy, but not stay in bed when he didn't feel like it.

It wasn't snowing. It was ridiculous for a man of more than fifty to go on being disappointed that there was no snow on Christmas morning, but middle-aged people are not always as dull and withered as the younger generation often think.

The sky, heavy and low and dirty white, seemed to weigh down on the roofs. Boulevard Richard-Lenoir was completely deserted and, directly opposite, above the wide main gate, the words 'Entrepôts Legal, Fils et Cie' were as black as boot polish. For some reason, the 'E' had a forlorn look about it.

He heard his wife moving about again in the kitchen, tiptoeing around the dining room, treading quietly without suspecting that he was up and standing looking out of the window. Glancing at his watch on the bedside table, he saw that it was ten minutes past eight.

The previous evening they had been to the theatre. Afterwards, they would have liked to have had something to eat in a restaurant, like everyone else, but everywhere all the tables had been booked up for the Christmas Eve festivities, and they had walked home instead, arm in arm. The result was that it was a little before midnight when they had got back, and they hadn't had long to wait before exchanging presents.

A pipe for him, as usual. For her, the latest model of a brand of electric coffee-maker which she had wanted plus, to remain true to tradition, a dozen finely embroidered handkerchiefs.

Automatically, he filled a fresh pipe. In some apartment blocks, on the other side of the boulevard, there were windows that had Venetian shutters and others that didn't. Not many people were up and about. Only here and there was a light burning, probably because there were children there who had woken up early so they could investigate the presents under the tree.

They would both spend a quiet morning cocooned in their apartment. Maigret would lounge around in his dressing gown until it was very late, without shaving, and go into the kitchen to chat with his wife as she was putting the lunch on the stove.

He didn't feel depressed exactly. It was just that his

dream – which he still could not remember – had left him with raw nerves. And anyway maybe it wasn't the dream but Christmas itself. He was going to have to tread carefully all day, weigh his words, just as Madame Maigret had calibrated her movements as she got out of bed, for she too would be a little more prickly than usual . . . But enough of that! Don't even think about it! Don't say a word that might bring up *that* subject. And later on, don't look out on to the street too often when the kids came out of doors and started showing off their toys.

There were children in most of the apartments, if not all. There would be the sound of tinny trumpets, drums, cap-guns . . . Little girls would already be playing with their dolls.

Once, a few years back, he had said, without really thinking:

'Why don't we make the most of Christmas and get away somewhere for a few days?'

'Get away where?' she had answered with unanswerable good sense.

Go and see who? They did not even have any family to visit, apart from her sister, who lived too far away. Go and stay in a hotel in some strange town or at an inn in the middle of nowhere?

Leave it! It was time to have his coffee and afterwards he would feel more himself. He was never fully at ease before that first of cup of coffee and his first pipe.

He was just reaching for the door handle when it opened soundlessly, and Madame Maigret appeared, holding a tray in her hand. She looked at the empty bed and then at him, disappointed, and on the verge of tears.

'You're up!'

With her hair done, she looked as fresh as a rose in her light-coloured apron.

'And there was me looking forward to bringing you breakfast in bed!'

He had many times tried, delicately, to make her understand that it wasn't a pleasure for him, that it made him feel uneasy, that it made him feel as if he were ill or helpless, but breakfast in bed continued for her to be the ideal treat for Sundays and public holidays.

'Sure you won't get back into bed?'

No! He couldn't face it.

'All right then . . . Happy Christmas!'

'Happy Christmas! . . . Are you cross with me?'

They were now in the dining room, with the silver tray on a corner of the table, steam rising from the cup of coffee and golden croissants in a napkin.

Putting his pipe down, he ate a croissant, just to humour her, but he remained standing as he looked out of the window:

'A dusting of snow.'

It wasn't really snow. A kind of fine white powder was falling and it reminded him that when he was little he used to stick his tongue out to catch the flakes.

His eye settled on the door of the building opposite, to the left of the warehouses. Two hatless women had just emerged from it. One, fair-haired and about thirty years of age, had thrown a coat over her shoulders, without putting her arms through the sleeves, while the other, who was older, was holding a shawl tightly round her.

The fair-haired one seemed to be hesitating, as if she was ready to turn and go back. The dark one, very small and thin, stood her ground, and Maigret had the feeling that she was pointing to his windows. Behind them, the concierge appeared in the doorway and seemed to be backing up the thin woman, and the blonde made up her mind to cross the road, not turning round, as if she was worried about something.

'What are you looking at?'

'Nothing . . . A couple of women . . .'

'What are they doing?'

'They look as if they're intending to come up here.'

Because both of them, now halfway across the boulevard, were looking up and were definitely staring in his direction.

'I hope they're not going to pester you on Christmas Day. I haven't even finished tidying the place up yet.'

Actually, no one would have noticed because, apart from the tray, nothing had been left lying around, and there was no dust dulling the sheen of the polished furniture.

'Are you sure they're coming here?'

'We'll soon find out.'

Just in case, he decided to run a comb through his hair, brush his teeth and splash a little water over his face. He was still in the bedroom, where he was relighting his pipe, when he heard a ring at the door. Madame Maigret must have shown her tough, protective side because a fair time went by before she came to find him.

'They insist on speaking to you,' she whispered. 'They said it could be important and need to ask your advice. I know one of them.'

'Which one?'

'The small, thin one, Mademoiselle Doncœur. She lives across the road, on the same floor as us. She sits working at her window all day. She's a very decent sort. She does delicate embroidery for a shop in Faubourg Saint-Honoré. I've sometimes wondered if she's not in love with you.'

'Why?'

'Because when you go out, she often stands up to get a better look at you.'

'How old is she?'

'Between forty-five and fifty. Aren't you going to put your suit on?'

Why should he not be entitled to wear a dressing gown when people came bothering him at home at half past eight on Christmas morning? Even so, he put on a pair of trousers under it then opened the door to the dining room, where both women stood waiting.

'I'm so sorry, ladies . . .'

Perhaps Madame Maigret had been right after all, because Mademoiselle Doncœur did not blush but turned pale, smiled, cancelled the smile but then turned it on again, opened her mouth but did not find anything to say.

On the other hand, the blonde was perfectly self-composed and, not without a hint of irritation, said:

'It wasn't me that wanted to come.'

'Perhaps you'd like to take a seat . . .'

He noticed that under her coat the blonde wasn't

dressed for company and wore no stockings, whereas Mademoiselle Doncœur was got up as if she were going to church.

'Maybe you are wondering how we had the nerve to come to see you,' the latter began, her words not coming easily. 'Like everyone hereabouts we know obviously who we are privileged to have as a neighbour . . .'

This time, her cheeks flushed a faint red. Then she looked at the tray.

'But we're stopping you finishing your breakfast.'

'I already finished. I'm all ears.'

'Something happened in our building this morning, or rather last night, something so disturbing that I immediately thought it was our duty to speak to you about it. Madame Martin didn't want to worry you. I said to her . . .'

'Do you live across the road too, Madame Martin?'

'I do, inspector.'

She was not happy, that much was patently obvious, at being pushed into coming here. But Mademoiselle Doncœur resumed where she had left off.

'We both live on the same floor, exactly opposite your windows (again she blushed, as if her statement was some sort of confession). Monsieur Martin is often away on business, which is understandable, since he is a commercial traveller. Their little girl has been in bed these last two months following a silly accident.'

Maigret turned to the woman with fair hair.

'You have a daughter, Madame Martin?'

'She's not actually our daughter, she's our niece. Her mother died just over two years ago, and ever since then the girl has lived with us. She broke her leg falling down-stairs. She should have got over it six weeks ago if there hadn't been complications.'

'Is your husband out of town at the moment?'

'He should be down in the Dordogne.'

'I'm all ears, Mademoiselle Doncœur.'

Madame Maigret had gone round by way of the bath-room to get back to her kitchen, where she could be heard rattling saucepans. From time to time, Maigret glanced out at the pale sky.

'This morning, I was up first thing, as usual, to go to first mass.'

'And did you go?'

'Oh yes! I got back about seven thirty, because I heard three masses. I got my breakfast ready. You might have seen the light in my window.'

He waved a hand to indicate that he hadn't been paying much attention.

'I couldn't wait to take a few sweeties and suchlike round for Colette. It's not a very happy Christmas for her. Colette is Madame Martin's niece.'

'How old is she?'

'Seven. That's right, isn't it, Madame Martin?'

'Seven in January.'

'At eight o'clock, I knocked on the door of the apartment.'

'I wasn't up,' said the blonde. 'Sometimes I sleep in quite late.'

'As I was saying, I knocked. Madame Martin kept me waiting for a minute or two, just enough time for her to slip on a dressing gown. I had my hands full and I asked her if I could give Colette her presents from me.

He sensed that the woman with fair hair had had time to examine everything in the apartment, though not without casting him an occasional pointed look tinged with suspicion.

'Then we both opened her bedroom door.'

'The child has a room to herself?'

'Yes. It's a two-bedroom apartment, with bathroom, dining room and kitchen. But I must tell you . . . No! I'll keep that for later. I'd got up to the moment when we opened the door. As it was dark inside, Madame Martin turned the light on.'

'Was Colette awake?'

'Yes. You could tell she hadn't been asleep for ages and was lying there, waiting. You know what children are like on Christmas morning! If she'd have been able to use her legs, she'd very likely have got up and gone to see what Father Christmas had brought her. Maybe another child would have called out. But she's already a young lady. You can tell she thinks a lot, that she's older than her years.'

Madame Martin now looked out of the window too, and Maigret tried to work out which apartment was hers. It had to be the one on the right, at the far end of the building, where two windows were lit.

Mademoiselle Doncœur went on:

'I wished her a happy Christmas. I said, and these are my exact words: "Look, sweetheart, at what Father Christmas left for you in my bedroom." '

Madame Martin's fingers twitched open and shut.

'And do you know what she replied without even looking at what I'd brought for her – actually they were just a few little things . . .?

'"I saw him."

'"Who did you see?"

'"Father Christmas."

'"When did you see him? Where?"

'"Here, last night. He came into my room."

'That's what she told us, isn't it, Madame Martin? Coming from another child, it would have made you smile, but I told you that Colette is already quite grown up. She wasn't joking.

'"How could you have seen him in the dark?"

'"He had a torch."

'"Did he put the light on?"

'"No. He had an electric torch. Look, Maman Loraine . . ."

'I should tell you that she calls Madame Martin *maman*, which is only natural, seeing as how her real mother is dead and Madame Martin has taken her place . . .'

All this was beginning to turn into a continuous, even drone in Maigret's ears. He had not yet drunk his second cup of coffee. His pipe had just gone out.

'Did she really see someone?' he asked, unconvinced.

'Oh yes, inspector. That's why I insisted that Madame Martin should come and speak to you. We've got proof. Colette gave a little knowing smile, pulled back the covers and showed us, in the bed, cuddled up close to her, a wonderful doll which hadn't been in the apartment the night before.'

'And you didn't give her the doll yourself, Madame Martin?'

'I was going to give her a doll, a much less glamorous one, that I bought yesterday afternoon in the Galeries. When we went into her room I was holding it behind my back.'

'So does this mean that last night someone did let himself into your apartment?'

'But that's not all,' Mademoiselle Doncœur broke in hurriedly, for she was now well launched. 'Colette isn't the sort of child who tells lies or plays tricks. Her mother and I questioned her. She is quite sure she saw someone dressed up like Father Christmas, with a white beard and wearing a full red suit.'

'At what time did she wake up?'

'She doesn't know. Some time in the night. She'd opened her eyes because she thought she saw a light, and there was indeed a light in the room. Part of the floor in front of the fireplace was lit up.'

'I have no idea of what it all means,' sighed Madame Martin, 'unless my husband knows more about it than I do.'

Mademoiselle Doncœur was determined to remain in control of the proceedings. The impression she gave was that it was she who questioned the child, leaving no detail unexplored, just as she had been the one who had thought of coming to see Maigret.

'Colette said Father Christmas was bending down on the floor, sort of crouching. And looked as if he was doing something.'

'And wasn't she scared?'

'No. She watched him and this morning she told us that he was making a hole in the floor. She thought that was how he was going to get into the apartment of the people below, the Delormes – they've got a little boy of three – and she also said the chimney was probably too narrow.

'The man must have sensed that he was being watched. Apparently he got up and approached the bed and put a great big doll on it, then held up one finger to his lips.'

'Did she see him leave?'

'Yes.'

'Through the floor?'

'No. Through the door.'

'Into what part of the apartment does that door lead?'

'It opens directly into the corridor outside. It's a room which used to be let separately. It has doors to both the apartment and the corridor.'

'Wasn't it locked?'

'It was,' said Madame Martin. 'I wasn't going to leave a child in an unlocked room.'

'Had the door been forced?'

'Probably. I don't know. Mademoiselle Doncœur insisted we come and see you at once.'

'Did you find a hole in the floor?'

Madame Martin shrugged, as if it was all too much for her, but Mademoiselle Doncœur answered for her.

'Not a hole exactly. But you could see that some of the boards had been lifted.'

'Tell me, Madame Martin, do you have any idea about what might have been under the floorboards?'

'No, inspector.'

'Have you lived in the apartment for long?'

'Ever since I got married, five years ago.'

'Was this room already part of the apartment?'

'Yes.'

'Do you know who lived there before you?'

'My husband. He's thirty-eight. When I married him he was thirty-three and living in his own place. Whenever he got back to Paris after one of his trips, he liked to feel that he'd come home.'

'You don't think he might have wanted to give Colette a surprise?'

'He's six or seven hundred kilometres from here.'

'Do you know where?'

'Bergerac, more likely than not. His itinerary is always planned in advance, and it's very unusual for him to depart from his schedule.'

'What line is he in?'

'He the rep for Zénith wristwatches for central and southwest France. It's a big firm, as you probably know. He's got an excellent job.'

'He's the nicest man on earth!' exclaimed Mademoiselle Doncœur, who then corrected herself, pink-cheeked:

'After you!'

'So, as I understand it, someone got into your apartment last night disguised as Father Christmas.'

'That's what Colette says.'

'And you heard nothing? Is your bedroom far from the child's?'

'The dining room is between the two.'

'You don't leave the intervening doors open at night?'

'There's no need. Colette isn't a nervous child and usually she never wakes up. If she needs to call me, she has a small brass bell on her bedside table.'

'Did you go out last night?'

'No, inspector,' she replied curtly, as if offended.

'Did you have any visitors?'

'I am not in the habit of having visitors when my husband is away.'

Maigret glanced up at Mademoiselle Doncœur, but she did not react, which suggested that the statement was most likely true.

'Did you go to bed late?'

'Straight away after they sang "O Holy Night" on the radio. Before that I'd been reading.'

'Did you hear anything unusual?'

'No.'

'Did you ask the concierge if she'd used the front door bolt-release from inside her lodge to let visitors in?'

Mademoiselle Doncœur pounced:

'I spoke to her about it. She said she hadn't.'

'And this morning, was anything missing from the apartment, Madame Martin?'

'No.'

'Who is with the child now?'

'No one. She's used to being on her own. I can't be at home all day. There's the shopping, errands to run . . .'

'I quite understand. Colette is an orphan, you said?'

'She has no mother.'

'So her father is still alive? Where is he now? Who is he?'

'He's my husband's brother, Paul Martin. As to telling you where he is . . .'

She gave a vague wave of her hand.

'When did you see him last?'

'At least a month ago. Longer ago than that. It was around All Saints' Day. He was completing a novena.'

'Excuse me?'

She replied with a hint of irritation:

'I might as well come straight out with it now, since we're having to get embroiled in our family problems.'

It was clear that she was cross with Mademoiselle Donc≈ur, whom she blamed for putting her in this situation.

'My brother-in-law, especially since he lost his wife, has stopped being much of a man.'

'What do you mean by that exactly?'

'He drinks. He used to drink before, but not to excess, and it didn't make him do stupid things. He had a regular job. In fact he had quite a good position in a furniture shop in Faubourg Saint-Martin, but after the accident . . .'

'His daughter's accident?'

'I mean the one that caused his wife's death. One Sunday, he had the brilliant idea of borrowing a friend's car and taking his wife and daughter out for a run out in the country. Colette was just a toddler.'

'When did this happen?'

'About three years ago. They went to have lunch in a riverside restaurant out somewhere near Mantes-la-Jolie. Paul couldn't resist their white wine, and it went to his head. When he got back into Paris, he was singing his head off, and the accident happened near the bridge at Bougival. His wife was killed instantly. His skull was cracked, and it was a miracle that he survived. Colette came out of it without a scratch. Ever since then, he hasn't amounted to much. We gave a home to their little girl. We have more or less adopted her. He comes to see her from time to time, but only when he is more or less sober. Then he backslides immediately . . .'

'Do you know where he lives?'

A vague movement of her hands.

'Here, there, everywhere. We have sometimes bumped into him shuffling about near Bastille, like a beggar. Sometimes he sells newspapers in the street. I'm saying all this in front of Mademoiselle Doncœur because unfortunately everyone in the building knows all about it.'

'You don't think he might have had the idea of coming to see his daughter dressed up like Father Christmas?'

'That's what I told Mademoiselle Doncœur. But she insisted that we should come and see you anyway.'

'Because he wouldn't have had any reason to go around lifting up floorboards,' Mademoiselle Doncœur retorted rather tartly.

'Maybe your husband came back to Paris earlier than expected and . . .'

'It's very likely something along those lines. I'm not worried. If it hadn't been for Mademoiselle Doncœur . . .'

Not again! Clearly she had not come across the boulevard gladly!

'Could you tell me where your husband might be staying?'

'The Hôtel de Bordeaux, in Bergerac.'

'Have you not thought of phoning him?'

'Nobody's on the phone in our building, except some people on the first floor, and they don't like being disturbed.'

'Would you have any objection if I phoned the Hôtel de Bordeaux?'

At first she acquiesced, then hesitated.

'He'll wonder what's happened.'

'You can speak to him.'

'He's not used to me phoning him.'

'Would you prefer not knowing?'

'No. All right, as you wish. I'll speak to him.'

He picked up the phone and asked to be connected. Ten minutes later, he had the Hôtel de Bordeaux on the line and handed the receiver to Madame Martin.

'Hello? I'd like to speak to Monsieur Martin, please. Jean Martin, yes . . . Never mind . . . Wake him . . .'

Cupping her hand over the receiver, she explained:

'He's still sleeping. They've gone to call him.'

She was visibly trying to work out what she was going to say.

'Hello? Is that you? . . . What? . . . Oh yes, happy Christmas! . . . Everything is fine, yes . . . Colette is fine . . . No, that's not only why I'm phoning . . . No no! Nothing serious, nothing to worry about . . .'

She repeated the words, separating each syllable:

'*I said nothing to worry about* . . . Except that last night something strange happened . . . Somebody dressed like Father Christmas got into Colette's bedroom . . . Of course not! He didn't harm her! . . . He gave her this enormous great doll . . . *Doll*, yes . . . And he fiddled about on the floor . . . He lifted up two floorboards, which he put back again quickly . . . Mademoiselle Doncœur said I should tell the police inspector who lives opposite us . . . I'm ringing you from his phone . . . You don't understand? . . . I don't either . . . Do you want to speak to him? I'll ask him . . .'

Turning to Maigret:

'He wants to speak to you.'

A firm but anxious voice at the other end of the line, the voice of a man who clearly didn't know what to think.

'Are you quite sure that no one has harmed my wife and little girl? . . . I am totally mystified! . . . If it was just the doll, I'd think it was my brother . . . Loraine will tell you all about him . . . She's my wife . . . Ask her to fill you in with the details . . . But he wouldn't have taken up floorboards just for fun . . . Do you think it would be best if I came back at once? I could get a train at about three this afternoon . . . What? . . . So I can count on you to look out for them? . . .'

Loraine took the receiver back.

'You see? The inspector is confident. He says there's definitely no danger. It's not worth interrupting your trip just when you are in line for that Paris-based promotion . . .'

Mademoiselle Doncœur was staring at her, and there was not much love lost in her eyes.

'I promise I'll phone or send you a wire if there's any news. She's quite happy. She's playing with the doll. I haven't had time yet to give her what you sent. I'll go and do it now . . .'

She hung up and said defiantly:

'There! Satisfied?'

Then after a brief silence:

'I'm very sorry for disturbing you. It wasn't my fault. I'm sure it's some silly practical joke, unless it's just something my brother-in-law dreamed up. When he's been drinking, you never know what he'll get up to next . . .'

'Aren't you expecting to see him today? Don't you think he'll want to come round to visit his daughter?'

'It all depends. If he's been drinking, no. He's always careful not to let her see him in that state. When he does come, he makes sure he's as presentable as possible.'

'May I ask you if you'll let me come round later and have a chat with Colette?'

'I've no reason to stop you. If you think it would do any good . . .'

'Thank you ever so much, Inspector Maigret,' exclaimed Mademoiselle Doncœur, with a glance that was both complicit and grateful. 'She is such an unusual little girl! You'll see!'

She retreated backwards to the door. A few moments later, Maigret saw them both crossing the boulevard one behind the other, Mademoiselle Doncœur stepping hard on Madame Martin's heels and turning round to glance up at the inspector's windows.

Onions were browning behind the kitchen door, which Madame Maigret now opened:

'Happy now?' she called softly.

Don't answer! Don't give any sign that you heard! It was Christmas morning and she must not be given any chance to dwell on the old couple that they had become, who had no one to spoil.

It was time he got shaved to go and see Colette.

2.

He had been halfway through his ablutions, just about to dunk his shaving brush in water, when he decided to phone. He hadn't bothered to put his dressing gown on; he was sitting in his pyjamas in the armchair in the dining room, his very own armchair, waiting for the call to be put through, watching the smoke rise slowly from all the chimneys.

To his ear, the ring tone at Quai des Orfèvres was unlike any other, and he felt he could see the wide, deserted corridors, the open doors of empty offices and the switchboard operator who would be calling Lucas, saying:

'It's the chief!'

He felt rather like one of his wife's friends for whom the greatest happiness – which she allowed herself to enjoy each and every day – was to spend the entire morning in bed, with windows shut and curtains closed, in the mellow glow of the night-light, calling up one or other of her friends on the off chance . . .

'Really! It's never at ten o'clock! What's the weather like? Raining? And you've already been out? You've done your shopping? . . .'

In this way, via the phone, she tried to capture echoes of the bustle of the world outside while nestling ever deeper into her comfortable, warm bed.

'Is that you, chief?'

Maigret would also have liked to ask Lucas who was on duty with him, what each of them was doing and what the place looked like that morning.

'Anything new? Not too overworked?'

'Not much happening. The usual things . . .'

'Look, I want you see if you can obtain some information for me. You should be able to get it by phone. First, get a list of men who have been released from prison in the last two months. Make it three months.'

'From which prison?'

'All of them. Don't worry about anybody sent down for five years or more. Try and find out if, among them, there was one who at some time in his life lived on Boulevard Richard-Lenoir. Got that?'

'I've made a note of it.'

Lucas must have been nonplussed but he did not let it show.

'Something else. We need to find a man named Paul Martin, a drunk, no fixed abode, often hangs out around Bastille. Don't arrest him. Leave him alone. Find out where he spent the night of Christmas Eve. The local police stations might be able to help.'

But unlike his wife's friend who loved phoning, it irked him to be at home, sitting in his armchair in pyjamas, his cheeks unshaven, staring out at a familiar, still cityscape where all that moved was the smoke from chimneys, while at the other end of the phone, the dependable Lucas had been on duty since six that morning and must already have unpacked his sandwiches.

'That's not quite all, old son. Call Bergerac. Hôtel de Bordeaux, there's a commercial traveller staying there named Jean Martin . . . No, Jean! It's not the same man. It's a brother. I'd like to know if sometime yesterday or during the night he got a phone call from Paris, or a wire. And while you're at it, you might as well ask where he spent yesterday evening. I think that's everything.'

'Want me to call you back?'

'Not straight away. I have to go out. I'll call you.'

'Has something happened down your way?'

'I don't know yet. Perhaps . . .'

Madame Maigret came into the bathroom to talk to him while he was finishing getting washed and shaved. Then, remembering the chimneys, he decided not to wear an overcoat. Just by looking at them, with their lazily rising smoke, which took ages to melt into the sky, he could imagine the overheated rooms behind those windows, and here he was, about to spend a long time in just such cramped accommodation where he would not be invited to make himself at home. He chose rather to cross the boulevard as if he was going to call on a neighbour, wearing just a hat.

The apartment building, like the one he himself lived in, was old but clean, yet a little forlorn, especially on that grey December morning. He did not stop to speak to the concierge, who felt rather slighted to see him walk straight by, and as he climbed the stairs doors silently opened a few inches as he passed, and he heard muffled footsteps and whisperings.

On the third floor, Mademoiselle Doncœur, who must

have been watching out of the window, was waiting for him in the corridor, feeling both somewhat overawed and very excited, as if this was a lovers' tryst.

'This way, Inspector Maigret. She went out some time ago.'

He frowned, and she noticed.

'I told her she was wrong, that you were coming, that it would be better if she stayed at home. She said she hadn't done her shopping yesterday, that there was no food in the house and that later on she wouldn't find any shops open. Come in.'

She was standing by a door at the end of the corridor. It led into a dining room, which was quite small and rather dark but clean and tidy.

'I'm babysitting until she comes back. Colette is looking forward to your visit, because I've told her all about you. Only she's a bit frightened in case you take her dolly off her.'

'When did Madame Martin decide to go out?'

'She started to get dressed immediately after we got back from seeing you.'

'Did she dress up specially?'

'I don't know what you mean.'

'I'd have thought that to go to the local shops she wouldn't dress in the same way as if she were going into town.'

'She was dressed up to the nines, with hat and gloves. She took a shopping bag with her.'

Before going in to Colette's room, Maigret paused to glance into the kitchen, where the remains of someone's breakfast had not been cleared away.

'Did she have breakfast before you two came to see me?'

'No. I didn't give her time.'

'Did she have breakfast after?'

'Not then either. She just made herself a cup of black coffee. I gave Colette her breakfast while Madame Martin was getting ready.'

On the sill of the window overlooking the courtyard was a food-safe. Maigret examined it closely and saw that it contained cold meat, butter, eggs and some vegetables. In the kitchen sideboard, he found two fresh loaves which had not been started. Colette had had croissants to eat with her hot chocolate.

'Do you know Madame Martin very well?'

'She's a neighbour, isn't she? I've seen more of her since Colette has been in bed, because she often asks me to look in on her when she goes out.'

'Does she go out often?'

'Not very often. Just to go shopping.'

He had been struck by something when he came in and was trying to pin it down, something in the atmosphere, in the way the furniture was arranged, in the kind of orderliness he found everywhere, and even in the smell of the place. It was by watching Mademoiselle Doncœur that he found, or thought he found, the answer.

Earlier, he had been told that Monsieur Martin had lived in the apartment before he got married. Now, despite the presence of Madame Martin for the past five years, it had remained a bachelor's apartment. For example, he pointed to two enlarged photos hanging on either side of the chimney.

'Who are they?'

'Monsieur Martin's father and mother.'

'Are there no photos of the parents of Madame Martin?'

'I've never heard her speak of them. I assume she doesn't have any family.'

Even the bedroom was plain, bereft of feminine touches.

He opened the wardrobe and next to masculine clothes carefully arranged he saw women's garments, mainly tailored suits and dresses in sober colours. He didn't dare open any drawers but he was sure they did not contain anything in the way of fripperies or those little trinkets which women usually collect.

A calm, small voice called: 'Mademoiselle Doncœur!'

'Let's go and see Colette,' he said

The child's bedroom was also austere, almost bare, with a bed that was too big for the grave-faced little girl who had curious, unguarded eyes.

'Are you the man who is a police inspector?'

'That's me, sweetheart. Don't be frightened.'

'I'm not frightened. Hasn't Maman Loraine come back yet?'

He was struck by the words. Hadn't the Martins more or less adopted their niece?

For the child had not said just 'Maman' but 'Maman Loraine'.

'Do you think that it was Father Christmas who came to see me last night?'

'I'm sure it was.'

'Maman Loraine doesn't think so. She never believes what I say.'

Her face looked drawn, her eyes were bright and the expression in them insistent. The plaster, which made one of her legs seem swollen all the way up to the top of her thigh, formed a small mountain under the bedclothes.

Mademoiselle Doncœur remained standing in the doorway and now, self-effacingly, so as to leave them alone together, she said:

'I'm just popping back to my apartment to make sure nothing's burning on the stove.'

Maigret, who had sat down by the bed, did not know where to start. He honestly had no idea of what question to ask first.

'Do you love your Maman Loraine?'

'Yes.'

She replied solemnly, without warmth, but also without hesitation.

'And your daddy?'

'Which one? Because I have two daddies, you know, Daddy Paul and Daddy Jean.'

'Is it very long since you saw Daddy Paul?'

'I don't know. Perhaps a few weeks. He promised to bring me a toy for Christmas but he hasn't come yet. He must have been ill.'

'Is he often ill?'

'Yes, often. When he's ill, he doesn't come to see me.'

'And what about Daddy Jean?'

'He's away travelling, but he's coming back for the New Year. Perhaps he will then be given a new job in Paris so he won't have to go away any more. He'd like that, and me too.'

'Have lots of friends been coming to see you since you've been in bed?'

'What friends? The little girls in my school don't know where I live. Or, if they do know, they're not allowed to come and see me by themselves.'

'What about the friends of Maman Loraine or your daddy?'

'Nobody ever comes.'

'Never? Are you sure?'

'Only the man from the gas or the electricity. I hear them because the door is almost always open. I know them. Somebody did come, but only twice.'

'A long time ago?'

'The first time was the day after my accident. I remember because the doctor had only just left.'

'Who was it?'

'I didn't see him. I heard him knock at the other door, and then talking, and Maman Loraine shut my bedroom door at once. They whispered for quite a long time. Afterwards, she told me he had come bothering her about an insurance policy. What's an insurance policy?'

'And did he come back?'

'Yes, about five or six days ago. This time, it was in the evening, when the light in my room had already been turned off. I hadn't gone to sleep yet. I heard someone knocking, then there was whispering like the first time. I knew straight away it wasn't Mademoiselle Doncœur, who sometimes comes in the evening to keep Maman

Loraine company. Later I thought they were quarrelling and I was frightened and I called and Maman Loraine came and told me that it was about the insurance thing again and that I should go to sleep.'

'Did he stay long?'

'I don't know. I think I must have gone to sleep.'

'Did you see him on either occasion?'

'No. But I'd know his voice again.'

'Even though he was whispering?'

'Yes. Especially because he was whispering, it made a sound like a big bumble bee. I can keep the doll, can't I? Maman Loraine bought me two boxes of sweets and a little sewing set. She bought me a doll too. It's not as big as the one from Father Christmas because she isn't very rich. She showed it to me this morning before she went out, then she put it back in the box, because I've got this one, so I don't need it. The shop will take it back.'

The apartment was overheated, and the rooms were small and stuffy. Yet Maigret suddenly felt a distinct chill. The apartment building was very like the one he lived in on the other side of the road. Was it him or did the people here seem blinkered and smaller-minded?

He bent down over the spot on the floor where the two boards had been lifted and saw nothing but the dusty cavity, slightly damp, that is found under floors everywhere. A few scratches in the wood showed that a chisel or something similar had been used.

He then examined the door and found signs that force had been used there too.

It was the work of an amateur, and it had not needed much doing.

'Wasn't Father Christmas cross when he saw you looking at him?'

'No. He was busy making a hole in the floor so he could go down to the little boy on the second floor.'

'Didn't he say anything?'

'I think he smiled. I'm not sure on account of his beard. It was quite dark. I'm certain he put one finger on his mouth, so that I wouldn't cry out, because grown-ups aren't allowed to see him. Have you ever seen him?'

'Oh, a very long time ago.'

'When you were little?'

He heard footsteps in the corridor. The door opened. It was Madame Martin wearing a grey suit and carrying a bag of provisions in one hand. She had a small beige hat on her head. She was visibly cold. The skin of her face looked tight and very pallid, but she must have been hurrying and run up the stairs, because two small red patches glowed in her cheeks and she was breathing hard.

She did not smile and asked Maigret:

'Has she been good?'

Then, as she took off her jacket:

'I'm so sorry for keeping you waiting. I had to go out to buy various things, and later on the shops would have been shut.'

'Did you meet anybody?'

'What do you mean?'

'Nothing. I just wondered if anybody had tried to speak to you.'

She had had enough time to go much further than Rue Amelot or Rue du Chemin-Vert, where most of the local shops were located. She could even have taken a taxi or the Métro and gone to almost any part of Paris.

All the tenants in the building must have been keeping their eyes and ears open, and Mademoiselle Donccœur put in an appearance, asking if they needed her. Madame Martin was obviously about to say no, but it was Maigret who answered:

'I'd like you to stay with Colette while I'm in the other room.'

She realized that he was asking her to keep the child occupied while he talked to Madame Martin. The latter also understood but gave no sign that she had.

'Come this way, please,' she said. 'You won't mind if I get rid of these things?'

She went in to the kitchen to put her shopping down, then removed her hat and fluffed up her straw-coloured hair. When the girl's bedroom door closed, she said:

'Mademoiselle Donccœur is in her element. This must be a godsend for an old spinster, mustn't it? Especially an old girl who collects newspaper articles about a certain police inspector who she has finally managed to get into the building where she lives! You don't mind, do you?'

She took a cigarette from a silver case, tapped one end and lit it with a lighter. Perhaps it was this action that prompted Maigret to ask her a question.

'You don't work, Madame Martin?'

'I'd find it hard to hold down a job and look after the

apartment and see to Colette, even though she goes to school now. In any case, my husband won't let me work.'

'But presumably you did work before you met him?'

'Of course. I had to earn my living. Wouldn't you like to sit down?'

He sat down on a straight-backed chair with a straw seat while she leaned one thigh against the table.

'Were you a shorthand typist?'

'I was.'

'Did you work for long?'

'Long enough.'

'Were you still working when you met Martin? I'm sorry but I have to ask you this question.'

'It's your job.'

'You got married five years ago. Where were you working at that time? Just a moment. May I ask how old you are?'

'I'm thirty-three. So I was twenty-eight and working for Monsieur Lorilleux in Palais Royal.'

'As a secretary?'

'Monsieur Lorilleux had a jewellery business, or rather a shop that sold souvenirs and collectable coins. You know those old curio shops in the Palais Royal. I did everything: shop assistant, secretary, served at the till. I looked after the place when he was out.'

'Was he married?'

'With three children.'

'Did you leave him to marry Martin?'

'Not exactly. Jean didn't like the idea of me going on working, but he was not earning all that much, and I had a steady job. So I went on with it for the first few months.'

'And afterwards?'

'Afterwards something happened that was low-key and quite unexpected. One morning, at nine o'clock, I turned up as usual at the door of the shop. It was locked. I waited, assuming that Monsieur Lorilleux was late.'

'He didn't live over the shop?'

'He lived in Rue Mazarine, with his family. At nine thirty, I started to worry.'

'Was he dead?'

'No. I phoned his wife, who told me he had left the apartment at eight o'clock, as usual.'

'Where did you phone from?'

'The glove shop next door. I waited all morning. His wife came over and joined me. We went together to the police, where, incidentally, no one took the matter very seriously. All they did was ask his wife if he had a weak heart, if he was having an affair, things like that. He was never seen or heard of again. The business was sold to some Poles, and my husband insisted I should stop working.'

'And how long was this after you'd got married?'

'Four months.'

'Was your husband already working as a rep in the southwest?'

'He already had the same area as he does now.'

'Was he in Paris when your employer disappeared?'

'No. I don't think so.'

'Did the police search the premises?'

'Nothing had been disturbed. The place was exactly as it had been left the night before. Nothing was missing.'

'Do you know what became of Madame Lorilleux?'

'She lived for a while on the money she got from the sale of the shop. Her children must be grown up by now and probably married. She's got a small haberdasher's shop these days not far from here, in Rue du Pas-de-la-Mule.'

'Have you kept in touch with her?'

'I've been in her shop a few times. As a matter of fact that's how I found out she had opened the business. The first time I went in I didn't recognize her.'

'How long ago was that?'

'I don't know. About six months.'

'Does she have a phone?'

'No idea. Why?'

'What sort of man was Lorilleux?'

'You mean to look at?'

'Start with a physical description.'

'He was tall, taller than you and even broader in the shoulder. He was a large man, but flabby, if you know what I mean, and he didn't take much care with his appearance.'

'Age?'

'About fifty, I don't know exactly. He had a small pepper-and-salt moustache, and his clothes were always too big for him.'

'Did you know much about his habits?'

'He used to walk to the shop every morning and arrived about a quarter of an hour before me, so that he'd finished sorting the mail by the time I got there. He didn't talk much. He was the melancholy type. He spent most of every day in the little office at the back.'

'Did he have affairs with women?'

'Not as far as I know.'

'Did he try to cosy up to you?'

Her reply was curt:

'No!'

'Did he rely much on you?'

'I believe he valued the work I did.'

'Did your husband ever meet him?'

'They never spoke to each other. Sometimes, Jean came to meet me outside the shop, but he kept a certain distance. Is that everything you wanted to know?'

There may have been a hint of impatience, even of anger, in her voice.

'May I remind you, Madame Martin, that it was you who came to me?'

'Only because that old bat seized the opportunity to get a closer look at you and almost forced me to go with her.'

'Don't you like Mademoiselle Doncœur?'

'I don't like people who stick their noses into what's none of their business.'

'Is that what she does?'

'We gave a home to my brother-in-law's child, as you know. You can believe me or not, but I've done my level best for her, I treat her as I would my own daughter.'

Again he had an instinctive feeling, an intuition, something ill-defined and insubstantial: stare as he might at the woman facing him, who had just lit another cigarette, he just could not see her as a mother.

'She comes here saying she wants to help but in fact she's forever nosing around in my affairs. If I go out for a few minutes, I meet her in the corridor, all sweetness, and she says:

'"You're not going to leave Colette all by herself are you, Madame Martin? Why don't you let me keep her company?"'

'I sometimes wonder if, when I'm out, she doesn't pass the time rummaging through my drawers.'

'But you put up with her.'

'Because I have no choice. Colette's the one who keeps asking for her, especially since she's been laid up in bed. My husband is also quite fond of her because before he married me he once had pleurisy, and she used to come and look after him.'

'Have you taken back the doll you bought for Colette's Christmas present?'

She frowned and glanced up at the communicating door.

'I see you have been asking her questions. No, I haven't taken it back for the very good reason that I bought it in a department store, and department stores are closed today. Would you like to see it?'

She said it defiantly and, contrary to her expectations, he allowed her to bring it, inspected the cardboard box from which the price, the very low price, had not been removed.

'May I ask where you went this morning?'

'Shopping.'

'Where? Rue du Chemin-Vert? Rue Amelot?'

'Rue du Chemin-Vert and Rue Amelot.'

'And what, forgive my asking, did you buy?'

Looking furious, she strode into the kitchen, came back with the bag of provisions and almost threw it on the table in the dining room.

'See for yourself.'

There were three tins of sardines, ham, butter, potatoes and a lettuce.

She watched him, stonily, unblinkingly, but without trembling and with more venom than apprehension.

'Got any other questions to ask me?'

'I would like to know the name of your insurance agent.'

She did not understand immediately, as was very clear. Then she tried to remember.

'My agent . . .'

'Insurance agent. The one who came here to see you.'

'I'm so sorry! I had forgotten. It's because you said *my* agent, as though I had a business relationship with whoever it was. It was Colette who told you that too. Actually somebody did come, one of those men who go round knocking on doors and are such hard work to get rid of. I thought at first that he was selling electric vacuum cleaners. In fact it was life insurance.'

'How long did he stay?'

'Just long enough for me to send him packing and make it very clear that I had no wish to sign any policy insuring my life or my husband's.'

'What company did he represent?'

'He did tell me, but I've forgotten. A name with the word "Mutual" in it.'

'And he came back and tried again?'

'Perfectly true.'

'At what time does Colette usually to go to sleep?'

'I turn out her light at half past seven, but sometimes she tells herself stories very quietly for quite a time after that.'

'So the second time, the insurance agent must have come to see you after seven thirty in the evening?'

She had already sensed the trap.

'Quite possibly. Actually, I was doing the washing-up.'

'And you let him in?'

'He had one foot in the door.'

'Did he knock on other residents' doors in the building?'

'I wouldn't know. I imagine you'll go and find out. Just because a little girl saw or thought she saw Father Christmas, you've been questioning me as though I'd committed a crime. If my husband were here . . .'

'Incidentally, does your husband have life insurance?'

'I think so. Yes he does.'

And as he was making his way to the door, after picking up his hat off a chair, she exclaimed, in surprise:

'Is that all?'

'That's all. If your brother-in-law comes to see you, as I gather he seems to have promised his daughter he would, I'd be most grateful if you would let me know or send him to see me. And now, I'd like to have a few words with Mademoiselle Doncœur.'

Mademoiselle Doncœur duly followed him along the corridor then overtook him and opened the door to her apartment, which smelled like a convent.

'Do go in, inspector. I hope it's not too untidy.'

Maigret saw no cat, no dog, no antimacassars on the furniture, no knickknacks on the mantelpiece.

'Have you been living in this apartment building for long, Mademoiselle Doncœur?'

'Twenty-five years, inspector. I am one of the oldest residents and I remember that when I first came, you were already living opposite and that you had a long moustache.'

'Who lived in the apartment next door before Martin moved in?'

'A civil engineer from the highways department. I don't remember his name but I could find it for you. He lived there with his wife and daughter, who was deaf and dumb. It was very sad. They left Paris and went to live in the country, somewhere near Poitiers, if I remember correctly. The man was old and must be dead by now because he had already reached retirement age.'

'Have you been bothered lately by a man selling insurance?'

'Not recently. The last time one came ringing at the door was at least two years ago.'

'You don't like Madame Martin, do you?'

'Why?'

'I'm asking if you like or do not like Madame Martin.'

'Well I tell you, if I had a son . . .'

'Go on.'

'If I had a son, I wouldn't be happy to have her for a daughter-in-law, especially since Monsieur Martin is such a nice, kind man!'

'You don't think he is happy with her?'

'I wouldn't say that. I haven't anything against her in particular. She is the way she is, there's no law against that.'

'What way is she?'

'I couldn't say. You've seen her. You know about such things better than I do. She isn't at all very womanly. For example, I'd bet she's never cried in her life. She brings up that little girl correctly, properly, it's true. But she never has a loving word for her, and, whenever I try to tell her fairy stories, I get the feeling it annoys her. I'm sure she's told her that Father Christmas does not exist. Fortunately Colette doesn't believe her.'

'And Colette doesn't like her either?'

'She does what she's told, tries her best to please her, but I think she's just as happy when she's left to herself.'

'Does Madame Martin go out a lot?'

'Not a lot. You can't criticize her for anything really. I don't know how to put it. You feel that she leads her own life regardless, if you know what I mean. She doesn't bother much with other people. She never talks about herself either. She is proper, proper all the time, too proper by half. She should have spent her life in an office, adding up figures or keeping an eye on the clerks.'

'Is that also the opinion of other residents?'

'She hardly has anything to do with them. It's as much as she can manage to say good morning to people when she meets them on the stairs. Actually, if we know her at all, it's only since Colette came, because people are always more interested in children.'

'Did you ever meet her brother-in-law?'

'In the corridor. I've never spoken to him. He walks right past you with his head bent as if he's ashamed and though he obviously goes to a lot of trouble to spruce himself up before coming, you always have the impression that he's slept in his clothes. I don't think it was him, inspector. He isn't the sort of man who'd do that. Or if he did, he must have been very drunk.'

Maigret made one last stop, at the concierge's door. Inside, it was so dark that the lights had to be kept on more or less all day. It was almost noon when he walked back across the boulevard, while all the curtains twitched in the windows of the building from which he had emerged. A curtain moved also in his own window. It was Madame Maigret watching out for him so that she could put the chicken in the oven. From where he was, he sent up a signal with a small wave of his hand and very nearly put out his tongue to catch one of those tiny granules of ice that drifted on the air, whose bland taste he could still remember.

3.

'I wonder if that little girl is happy,' sighed Madame Maigret as she got up from table to bring the coffee from the kitchen.

She saw that he was not listening. He had pushed his chair back and was filling his pipe as he watched the stove, which purred softly, its small, steady flames licking at the mica window at the front. But for her own satisfaction, she added:

'I don't think she can be, not with that woman.'

He smiled at her vaguely, the way he always did when he did not know what she had just said, then returned to contemplating the salamander. There were at least ten similar stoves in the building, all purring in the same way, ten dining rooms filled with the same Sunday smell. It was doubtless also the case in the building opposite, with each apartment harbouring its own indolent, secret, muted life, with wine on the table, cakes, the small decanter of liqueur which would be brought out from the sideboard, while all the windows admitted the hard, grey light of a sunless day.

It was perhaps that which, though he did not know it, had been wrong-footing him all morning.

Nine times out of ten, an investigation, a serious one, would propel him from one minute to the next into a new environment, bringing him face to face with people from a world he did not know or knew only slightly, and which he would have to familiarize himself with even down to the minor habits and idiosyncrasies of a class which was alien to him.

But with this case, if it really was a case, for he had not been formally ordered to undertake an official investigation, it was all very different. For the first time, an incident had occurred in a world close to his own, in a block of apartments which could have been his.

The Martins might well have been living on his landing instead of opposite, and it was very likely that Madame Maigret would have been the one babysitting Colette while her aunt was out. On the floor above, there was an elderly unmarried lady who was a plumper, paler version of Mademoiselle Doncœur. The frames of the pictures of Martin's mother and father were exactly the same as those holding the photos of Maigret's parents and the enlargements had probably been done by the same photographic studio.

Was that the reason why he felt constrained? He had a sense of being too close, that he was not seeing people and things with a sufficiently fresh, new eye.

He had told his wife all about what he had been doing that morning as they ate – a very good little festive meal which had left him feeling bloated – and she had not stopped glancing out at the windows opposite with an uneasy expression on her face.

'Is the concierge quite sure no one could have come in from outside?'

'She isn't as sure as she was. She had friends round who

stayed until half past midnight. After that she went to bed, and there was an amount of coming and going as there always is on Christmas Eve.'

'Do you think anything else will happen?'

It was precisely that niggling thought that worried him. First, there was the fact that Madame Martin had not come to him spontaneously but had her arm twisted by Mademoiselle Doncœur.

If she had got up earlier, if she had been the first to discover the doll and hear the story about Father Christmas, would she have kept quiet and told the little girl not to say anything?

Then later she had taken the first opportunity to go out, although there was more than enough food in the house for that day. She had even absentmindedly bought butter when there was a pound left in the food-safe.

He got up and moved to his armchair by the window. He picked up the phone and called Quai des Orfèvres.

'Lucas?'

'I did what you asked, chief, and I have a list of all prisoners released in the last four months. There aren't as many as you might think. I haven't found one who has lived on Boulevard Richard-Lenoir at any given moment.'

That wasn't important now. Maigret had almost abandoned that line of inquiry. Anyway the theory was only a shot in the dark, the idea that someone living in the apartment opposite might have hidden the proceedings of a robbery or crime there before getting caught. When he was released, his first thought would naturally have been to get his hands on the loot. But because of Colette's accident, which kept her confined to her bed, the room was not empty at any hour of the day or night.

Acting the part of Father Christmas in order to get in without running any risk would not have been such a bad idea.

But if that had been the case, Madame Martin would not have hesitated to come to him for help. Nor would she have gone out straight afterwards using such a poor excuse.

'Would you like me to go through each case separately?'

'No. Got anything on Paul Martin?'

'I didn't have far to look. He is known in four or five police stations at least between Bastille, Hôtel de Ville and Boulevard Saint-Michel.'

'Do you know what he did last night?'

'First, he went and had something to eat on board the Salvation Army barge. He goes there every week, on his day, like the other regulars and on those evenings he is sober. They were serving Christmas dinners. He had to queue up for it for quite a long time.'

'What did he do next?'

'At around eleven, he went to the Latin Quarter and opened car doors for people outside a nightclub. He must have made enough to go drinking, because around four in the morning he was picked up dead drunk about a hundred metres from Place Maubert. He was taken to the local lock-up. He was still there this morning at eleven o'clock. He'd just been let out when I got this information, but they promised they'd bring him here to me as soon as they found him. He still had a few francs left in his pocket.'

'Bergerac?'

'Jean Martin is getting the first afternoon train. He seemed very surprised and very concerned by the phone call he got this morning.'

'Did he have any visitors?'

'This morning, yes. But someone had phoned last night just as he was sitting down in the hotel restaurant.'

'Did you find out who called him?'

'The woman at the desk who took the call says it was a man's voice. He asked if Jean Martin was there. She sent one of the waitresses to get him, and when he came to the phone there was no one at the other end. It spoiled his evening. There were several of them, all commercial travellers, who had organized a visit to some club or other in the town. I was given to understand that there were pretty girls with them. It seems that Martin, after he'd had a few drinks to be sociable, talked all the time about his wife and daughter, because he calls the kid his daughter. But that did not prevent him staying out with his friends until three in the morning. Is that everything you wanted to know, chief?'

Lucas, who was curious, could not prevent himself adding:

'Has a crime been committed in your part of town? Are you still at home?'

'Up to now it's just something and nothing about Father Christmas and a doll.'

'Oh!'

'Just a moment. I want you to try and get the address of the head of Zénith the watchmakers in Avenue de l'Opéra. You should be able to find it even on a public holiday, and there's a good chance he'll be at home. Will you call me back?'

'As soon as I have the information.'

His wife had brought him a glass of sloe-gin. Her sister in Alsace sent them a bottle from time to time. He gave her a smile and for a moment was tempted not to think any more about this absurd business and to suggest that they go out and spend a quiet afternoon at the cinema.

'What colour are her eyes?'

He had to make an effort to work out that she meant the little girl, who was the only one in the whole story who interested Madame Maigret.

'You know, I'd find it hard to say. They're certainly not brown. She's got fair hair.'

'So they must be blue, then.'

'Maybe. But light-coloured, at any rate. And calm, especially.'

'Because she doesn't look at things the way children normally do. Did she laugh?'

'There was no reason for her to laugh.'

'A real child will always find a reason to laugh. All it takes is for her to feel safe and be allowed think as children of her age do. I don't like that woman!'

'Do you prefer Mademoiselle Doncœur?'

'An old spinster she might be, but I'm sure she knows more about dealing with the little girl than this Martin woman. I've met her in shops. She is one of those women who watch when shopkeepers weigh things and count out their money coin by coin from the bottom of their purses and look around suspiciously as if everyone was trying to rob them.'

She was interrupted by the ringing of the telephone, but she found time to repeat:

'I don't like the woman.'

It was Lucas, who gave him the address of Arthur Godefroy, the general agent for Zénith Watches in France. He lived in a very large house at Saint-Cloud and Lucas confirmed that he was at home."

'And Paul Martin is here, chief.'

'They delivered him to you?'

'Yes. He's wondering why. Wait a second while I close the door . . . Right! Now he can't hear me. At first he thought something had happened to his daughter and started crying. He's calm now, resigned, and he's got a terrible hangover. What do I do with him? Want me to send him to you?'

'Have you got anyone who could bring him here?'

'Torrence has just come in and would like nothing better than a breath of air because I think he was out celebrating last night too. Anything else you need me to do?'

'Yes. Contact the station at Palais Royal. About five years ago, a man named Lorilleux, who had a shop there selling jewellery and old coins, disappeared without trace. I'd like to have all they've got on the case.'

He smiled as he glanced up and saw that his wife opposite him had returned to her knitting. This inquiry was turning into quite a family affair.

'Shall I call you back?'

'I'm not thinking of going anywhere.'

Five minutes later, he had Monsieur Godefroy, who had a very strong Swiss accent, on the other end of the line.

When the name of Jean Martin was mentioned, he thought at first, since he was being disturbed on Christmas Day, that his employee must have had an accident and spoke of him in the most glowing terms.

'He is such a conscientious and capable man that next year, that is two weeks from now, I have decided to keep him at my side here in Paris as my deputy. Do you know him? Do you have a serious reason for taking an interest in him?'

He told children in the background to be quiet.

'Sorry about that. All the family are here together and . . .'

'Tell me, Monsieur Godefroy, do you know if anyone recently, in the last few days, has contacted your office to ask about Monsieur Martin's current whereabouts?'

'I do indeed.'

'Could you give me a few details?'

'Yesterday morning, someone rang my office and asked to speak to me personally. I was very busy, because of the holiday period. They must have given a name, but I've forgotten it. They wanted to know where Jean Martin could be contacted because they had an urgent message for him. I had no reason not to say that he was in Bergerac, probably at the Hôtel de Bordeaux.'

'Didn't they ask anything else?'

'No. Whoever it was hung up straight away.'

'Thank you so much.'

'Are you sure that there's nothing in this matter that I should worry about?'

The children must have been climbing all over him, and Maigret saw his chance to say a hasty goodbye.

'Did you hear that?'

'I heard what you said, of course, but not what he replied.'

'Yesterday, a man phoned his office to find out where Jean Martin was. No doubt the same man phoned Bergerac yesterday evening to make sure he was still there and would not be anywhere near Boulevard Richard-Lenoir on the night before Christmas.'

'And was he the man who broke into the apartment?'

'More than likely. At the very least, it proves that the intruder was not Paul Martin, who would not have needed to make those two telephone calls. He could have found out from his sister-in-law without making it obvious.'

'You're starting to get excited. Don't deny it, you're only too happy that this business has happened today.'

And, as he looked for an excuse:

'Go on, it's only natural! I'm curious too. For how much longer do you think the little girl will have to stay with her leg in plaster?'

'I never asked.'

'I'm just wondering what the complication could have been.'

Once more she had unwittingly started Maigret's mind moving in a new direction.

'What you just said is really quite interesting.'

'What did I say?'

'Actually, since she's been in bed for two months, there's every chance, unless there are further, really serious complications, that she won't be laid up for much longer.'

'She'll probably have to walk with crutches to start with.'

'That's not the point. The point is that in a few days, a few weeks at the most, the child will leave her room, and there will be times when she'll go out for walks with Madame Martin. The coast will be clear, and it will be easy for anyone to get into the apartment without having to dress up as Father Christmas.'

Madame Maigret's lips were working because, while she listened with her eyes calmly on her husband, she was counting her stitches.

'First, it was Colette's presence in the room that forced the man to resort to subterfuge. She'd been in bed for two months. So it could be that he'd been waiting for two months. If it had not been for the complications which had slowed her convalescence, the floorboards could have been taken up about three weeks ago.'

'Where is all this leading?'

'Nowhere. Or rather, I'm wondering if the man couldn't wait any longer and had pressing reasons to act without further delay.'

'In a few days, Martin will be back from his trip.'

'That's true.'

'What could the intruder have found under the floorboards?'

'But did he actually find anything? If he didn't find any-thing, his problem is still as urgent as it was yesterday. So he'll try again.'

'How?'

'I have no idea.'

'Listen, Maigret, aren't you afraid for that little girl? Do you think she is safe with that woman?'

'I could answer that if I knew where Madame Martin went this morning when she said she'd gone shopping.'

Picking up the phone, he dialled the Police Judiciaire one more time.

'It's me again, Lucas. This time I want you to find out about taxis. I'd like to know if anyone picked up a fare, a woman, on or around Boulevard Richard-Lenoir between nine and ten o'clock this morning, and where she was taken. Wait a second! . . . Yes, I'm thinking about it . . . She has fair hair, looks early thirties, on the thin side but sturdy enough. She was wearing a grey tailored suit and a small beige hat. She was carrying a bag of provisions. There can't have been many cars on the roads this morning.'

'Has Martin arrived?'

'Not yet.'

'He won't be long now. About the other man, Lorilleux, the Palais Royal colleagues are searching their records. You'll have the information soon.'

It was about now that Jean Martin was getting on the train in Bergerac. Little Colette was most likely having her afternoon nap. Mademoiselle Doncœur's silhouette could be made out behind her curtains. She was probably wondering what Maigret was doing.

People began emerging from their apartment buildings, especially families with children who were trailing their new toys along the pavement. There would certainly be queues outside cinemas. A taxi drew up. Then footsteps were heard on the stairs. Madame Maigret went to open the door even before anyone had time to ring the bell. Then Torrence's loud voice saying:

'Are you there, chief?'

And into the room he ushered a man of indeterminate age who stood self-effacingly against the wall and kept his eyes fixed on the floor.

Maigret got a couple of glasses from the sideboard and filled each with sloe-gin.

'Here you are,' he said.

The man's trembling hand faltered, and he looked up with surprised, anxious eyes.

'Your very good health, Monsieur Martin. I'm sorry I have dragged you all the way here, but at least it's nearer for you to go and see your daughter.'

'Has something happened to her?'

'No, nothing. I saw her this morning, and she was playing quietly with her new doll. You can go now, Torrence. Lucas must have work for you to do.'

Madame Maigret, taking her knitting with her, made herself scarce and settled in the bedroom where she sat down on the edge of the bed, still counting stitches.

'Do have a seat, Monsieur Martin.'

The man had merely taken a sip from his glass before putting it down on the table, but from time to time kept darting worried glances in its direction.

'There's absolutely nothing for you to worry about, I'm fully acquainted with your past, you know.'

'I wanted to go and see her this morning,' sighed the man. 'I'd sworn I'd go to bed, get up early and come and wish her happy Christmas.'

'I know that too.'

'It always happens the same way. I swear I'll just have one drink, to set me up . . .'

'You have only one brother, Monsieur Martin?'

'Jean, yes, he's six years younger than me. Along with my wife and daughter, he's all I love in the whole world.'

'Don't you care much for your sister-in-law?'

Taken aback, he gave a start and looked uneasy.

'I haven't got anything bad to say about Loraine.'

'You gave your daughter into her keeping, didn't you?'

'Well, the fact is, when my wife died and I started to go off the rails . . .'

'I understand. Is your daughter happy?'

'I think so. She never complains.'

'Have you never tried to make a new start?'

'Every night I promise to be done with this way of living, and then next morning it all starts up again. I even went to see a doctor who gave me some advice.'

'Did you take it?'

'I did, for a couple of days. When I went back to see him, he was in a hurry. He said he didn't have time to treat me and thought I'd be better off going into a specialized clinic . . .'

He reached for his glass, then hesitated. So that he would feel free to have a drink, Maigret drained his own glass.

'Did you ever find any other men in your sister-in-law's apartment?'

'No, and I don't think anything can be said against her on that score.'

'Do you know where your brother met her?'

'In a small restaurant in Rue de Beaujolais where he always ate when he was in Paris between trips. It wasn't far from his office and near the shop where Loraine worked.'

'Did they have a long engagement?'

'I don't rightly know. Jean went away for two months and when he got back told me he was getting married.'

'Were you your brother's witness?'

'Yes. And Loraine chose as her witness the woman who ran the apartment building where she was living at the time. She has no family in Paris. She'd already lost her father and mother in those days. Is there something wrong . . .?'

'I don't know yet. Last night a man disguised as Father Christmas got into Colette's room.'

'Did he hurt her?'

'He gave her a doll. When she opened her eyes he was busy lifting two floorboards.'

'Do you think I'm presentable enough to go and see her?'

'You can go in a moment. If you think you should, you can have a shave here, brush yourself down a bit. Is your brother the kind of man who would hide anything under floorboards?'

'Him? Never!'

'Not even if there was something he wanted to hide from his wife?'

'He doesn't hide anything from her. You don't know him. When he gets back he shows her his expenses just like he would submit them to his boss and she always knows exactly how much money he has in his pocket.'

'Is she a jealous sort?'

The man did not answer.

'It would be best if you told me what you think. Come on, this is about your daughter.'

'I don't think Loraine is particularly jealous, but she likes money. At least, that's what my wife used to say. My wife didn't like her.'

'Why?'

'She used to say her lips were too thin, that she was too cold, too polite, that she was always on the defensive. According to her, she had thrown herself at Jean on account of his job, his furnished flat, his future . . .'

'Was she poor?'

'She never talks about her family. However we did find out that her father died when she was very young and that her mother cleaned people's houses.'

'In Paris?'

'Somewhere in the Glacière neighbourhood. That's why she never mentions that part of town. Like my wife said, she's someone who knows what she wants.'

'Was she, in your opinion, the mistress of her former employer?'

Maigret poured him a slug of the gin, and the man gave him a grateful look but hesitated, thinking no doubt of the visit to his daughter and his breath.

'I'll make you a cup of coffee. Your wife must have had an opinion about that, didn't she?'

'How do you know that? She never said anything nasty

about people, you know. But with Loraine it was almost a physical thing. Whenever we went to meet my sister-in-law, I used to beg my wife not to let her feelings and dislike show. It's funny, me talking to you about all this given the way I am. Perhaps I did a bad thing leaving Colette with her?'

'You haven't answered my question about Loraine's former employer.'

'Yes. My wife thought they looked as if they were having an affair and that it suited Loraine to marry a man who was away travelling most of the time.'

'Do you know where she lived before her marriage?'

'In a street just off Boulevard Sébastopol, first on your right when you go from Rue de Rivoli towards the main Boulevards. I remember because it was there that we went to fetch her by car on the day she got married.'

'Rue Pernelle?'

'That's it. The fourth or fifth building on the right is an apartment building with furnished rooms. It looks quiet, respectable, and people who live there tend to work nearby, including, I remember, small-time actresses from the Châtelet theatre.'

'Would you like to shave, Monsieur Martin?'

'I feel ashamed. But seeing that I'm here opposite where my daughter lives . . .'

'Come with me.'

He took him through the kitchen to avoid going via the bedroom occupied by Madame Maigret and gave him everything he needed, including a clothes brush.

When her husband returned to the dining room, Madame Maigret opened the door slightly and whispered:

'What's he doing?'

'Having a shave.'

Again he reached for the phone. The dependable Lucas was there, and he gave him a job to brighten up his Christmas Day.

'Can they spare you from the office?'

'Yes, if Torrence stays here. I've got that information you asked me for.'

'Hold that for a moment. I want you to go to Rue Pernelle, where you'll find a small hotel with furnished rooms, it is probably still there. I seem to think I've already seen it, it's one of the first buildings you come to just off Boulevard Sébastopol. I don't know if the owners are still the same as five years ago. Perhaps you can find somebody who worked there then. I'd be glad of anything you can get about a woman named Loraine . . .'

'Loraine who?'

'Wait a moment. I hadn't thought of that.'

Maigret made his way to the bathroom and, through the door, asked Martin what his sister-in-law's maiden name was.

'Boitel!' came the reply.

'Lucas? Her full name was Loraine Boitel. The woman who ran the apartment house was her witness when she married Martin. Loraine Boitel was working for Lorilleux at the time.'

'The same as the one from the Palais Royal?'

'Yes. I'm wondering if there was anything else between them and if he sometimes came to see her at her apartment. That's the lot. As quick as you can, now. It could be more urgent than we think. Now, what was it you wanted to tell me?'

'The Lorilleux case. He was a strange man. There was an investigation at the time he disappeared. In Rue Mazarine, where he lived with his family, he was regarded as a respectable shopkeeper who was an excellent father to his three children. In his shop in the Palais Royal some odd things went on. He didn't only sell souvenirs of Paris and old coins, but obscene books and prints too.'

'It's a local speciality.'

'Yes, but they're not even very sure that nothing else went on there. There are references to a wide divan upholstered with red rep which was found in the office at the back of the shop. There was no evidence, and the matter was not followed up, especially since no one wanted to trouble the customers who were, for the most part, more or less important men.'

'What about Loraine Boitel?'

'She's hardly mentioned in the report. She was already married at the time of Lorilleux's disappearance. She waited all morning in the shop doorway. It doesn't seem that she saw him the previous evening after they'd closed for the day. I was phoning about that point when Langlois from the Fraud Squad walked into my office. He pricked up his ears when he heard Lorilleux's name, said it rang a bell and went off to check in his files . . . Still there? It's nothing definite, just the fact that at around that time Lorilleux had been flagged up as someone who crossed the Swiss border frequently. It was when gold-trafficking was at its height. They kept an eye on him. He was searched two or three times at the frontier, but nothing was found.'

'Get yourself over to Rue Pernelle, Lucas. I'm more convinced than ever now that this is urgent.'

Paul Martin, pale-cheeked, close-shaven, was standing in the doorway.

'I'm embarrassed. I don't know how to thank you.'

'You're going to see your daughter, aren't you? I don't know how long you usually stay with her, nor how you're going to arrange it. But what I would like would be for you not to leave the apartment until I get there.'

'But I can hardly stay there all night.'

'Stay there all night if necessary. Just find a way.'

'Is there any danger?'

'I have no idea, but your place is with Colette.'

The man gulped down his black coffee and started making his way towards the stairs. The door was already closed again when Madame Maigret returned to the dining room.

'He can't go and see his daughter empty-handed. Not on Christmas Day.'

'But . . .'

Maigret started to reply, no doubt, that there weren't any dolls lying about in the apartment, when she held out a small shiny object, a gold thimble which had been in her sewing box for years. She never used it any more.

'Give him this. It's the sort of thing little girls always like. Go on, hurry up!'

From the top of the stairs, he called out:

'Monsieur Martin! . . . Monsieur Martin! . . . One moment, please!'

He slipped the thimble into his hand.

'But don't tell her where you got it, will you?'

On the threshold of the dining-room door, he paused grumpily. Then he sighed:

'Have you finished making me behave like Father Christmas?'

'I bet she'll prefer that to the doll. Because it's such a grown-up thing. You do understand that?'

They watched the man cross the boulevard, pause a moment in front of the apartment house, turn and glance up at Maigret's windows as if he were looking for a sign of encouragement.

'Do you think he'll ever stop drinking?'

'I doubt it.'

'If something happened to that woman, Madame Martin . . .'

'Go on.'

'Oh, nothing. I'm thinking of the little girl. I wonder what will become of her . . .'

Ten minutes at least ticked by. Maigret had opened a newspaper. His wife had resumed her place in the chair opposite him and was knitting, counting her stitches, when, blowing out a cloud of tobacco smoke, he growled:

'You've never even seen the kid.'

4.

Later, in the drawer where Madame Maigret regularly tidied away any stray pieces of paper, Maigret would come across an old envelope on the back of which, at various times that day, he had automatically jotted down events as they happened. It was only then that he was struck by something about this case, which he had conducted almost from beginning to end from his own apartment and which he would subsequently quote as an example.

Contrary to what so often happens, no unequivocal intervention of chance, no dramatic turning point was involved. That kind of chance had no part in events, and yet chance was nevertheless a factor, a constant presence, in the sense that every piece of information came at the right time and in the most straightforward, natural way.

Sometimes dozens of inspectors will work day and night gathering background information. For example, Arthur Godefroy, Zénith Watches' representative in France, could easily have spent the Christmas holidays in Zurich, where he was born. He might well simply not have been at home. Or again, it was highly possible that he might have had no knowledge of the phone call about Jean Martin which had been made to his office on Christmas Eve.

When Lucas got there a little after four o'clock, his nose

red and the skin tight on his face, the same effect had worked in his favour.

Thick yellowish fog had suddenly blanketed Paris, which is quite rare. The lights were on in all the buildings; from one end of the boulevard to the other, all of the windows looked like distant ships' lanterns; the details of everyday reality were blurred to the point where, had they been at the sea's edge, passers-by would have expected to hear the boom of a foghorn.

For one reason or another – probably it was prompted by a childhood memory – all that gave Maigret a certain pleasure, as it did to see Lucas walk into his apartment, remove his overcoat, sit down and hold out his frozen hands to the fire.

Lucas was virtually a replica of him, only a head shorter, with shoulders half as wide and a face to which he had some difficulty imparting a semblance of severity. Without making it obvious, or maybe through unconscious mimicry and admiration, he had come to copy even his chief's smallest gestures in his own body language and expressions, and it was more striking here than it was in the office – even down to the way he inhaled the fumes of the sloe-gin in his glass before he sipped its contents . . .

The woman who used to manage the apartment building in Rue Pernelle had died two years before in a Métro accident, which might have complicated the investigation. The staff of establishments of this kind tend to come and go, and there was little hope of finding anyone still working there who had known Loraine five years earlier.

But their luck held. Lucas had found that the current manager had been the old night caretaker and, as chance would have it, he had in the past been in trouble with the law, specifically the Vice Squad.

'That meant it was easier to make him talk,' said Lucas as he lit a pipe that was too big for him. 'I was surprised he should have had enough cash to buy the business outright, but in the end he explained he was the front man for someone in the public eye who invests his money in businesses of that kind but does not wish to have his name connected with them.'

'What sort of place is it?'

'Respectable from the outside. Quite clean. An office on the mezzanine. Rooms let by the month, a few by week. And also, on the first floor, rooms for rent by the hour.'

'Does he remember our young woman?'

'Very clearly, because she lived there for more than three years. I finally realized that he did not like her because she was very tight with her money.'

'Did Lorilleux come to see her there?'

'Before going to Rue Pernelle, I called in at the Palais Royal station to get a photo which was in the case file. I showed it to the manager. He recognized him at once.'

'Did Lorilleux call to see her often?'

'On average two or three times a month, and he always had luggage with him. He would come at around one thirty in the morning and leave again at six. At first I wondered what that could mean. I checked the railway timetable. The times coincided with the journeys he made to Switzerland. For his return, he would take the train which arrives in the middle of the night and allowed his wife to think that he'd taken the one that gets in at six in the morning.'

'Anything else?'

'Nothing, except that Loraine was not a generous tipper and that, contrary to the house rules, she cooked for herself in the evening in her room on a spirit stove.'

'Any other men?'

'No. With the exception of Lorilleux, she led an orderly life. When she married, she asked the manager's wife to stand as her witness.'

Maigret had had to twist his wife's arm to make her stay in the room, and she sat there in silence, as if she hoped they would forget all about her.

Torrence was outside, in the fog, going from one taxi stand to the next. The two men waited patiently, each sunk in an armchair, in identical poses, with a glass of spirits within reach. Maigret started to feel drowsy.

It was with the taxis as it had been with the rest. Sometimes the taxi being sought is the one you happen on straight away. At other times, whole days can go by without producing a result, especially when the vehicle being sought does not belong to a company fleet. Some drivers do not work regular hours, and just cruise around for such fares as they can pick up, and there is no guarantee that they see appeals for information made by the police in the newspapers.

Be that as it may, just before five o'clock, Torrence phoned from Saint-Ouen.

'I've found one of the taxi-drivers,' he said.

'Why *one*? Were there several?'

'I have good reasons for assuming so. He picked up the young woman this morning at the corner of Boulevard Richard-Lenoir and Boulevard Voltaire and dropped her in Rue de Maubeuge, close by Gare du Nord. She did not tell him to wait.'

'Did she go into the station?'

'No. She stopped outside a shop selling travel goods that stays open on Sundays and public holidays. The driver then lost interest in her.'

'Where is he now?'

'Here. He's just come back.'

'Would you send him round to see me? He can either come in his own cab or get another, but he must come as soon as possible. And you still have to find the driver who took her back home.'

'Understood, chief. I'll get on it after I've had a coffee with a little something in it for the cold, because it's freezing out here.'

Maigret glanced out across the road and saw a shadow in Mademoiselle Doncœur's window.

'Get the phone book and find me the number of a shop opposite Gare du Nord that sells travel goods.'

It took Lucas only a few moments, and Maigret dialled:

'Hello? Police Judiciaire here. You had a customer in this morning, a woman, just before ten, who will have bought something, a suitcase most likely. A young woman with fair hair, in a grey tailored suit, carrying a bag of shopping. Do you remember her?'

Was it perhaps the fact that it was Christmas Day which made everything easier? There were fewer cars about, and business was virtually non-existent.

Furthermore, people tend to remember more clearly things that happen on a day that is different from other days.

'I served her myself. She said she had to travel at short notice to Cambrai, to see her sister who was ill, and that she didn't have time to go home first. She wanted a cheap fibre case, like the ones we have displayed in piles on each side of the door. She chose one of moderate size, paid for it and went into the bar next door. A little while later, I was standing in the doorway of my shop when I saw her heading into the station carrying the case.'

'Are you by yourself in the shop?'

'There's a sales assistant with me.'

'Could you manage to get away for half an hour? Just get into a taxi and come and see me at this address . . .'

'I assume you will pay for the cab? Should I keep it waiting?'

'Yes, keep the taxi.'

According to the notes scribbled on the envelope, it was 5.30 p.m. when the driver of the first taxi arrived, rather taken aback, given that it was police business, to be summoned to a private address. But he recognized Maigret and looked curiously around him, visibly fascinated to see the home of the famous detective chief inspector.

'I want you to enter the building just opposite and go up to the third floor. If the concierge stops you on the way, say that you are going to see Madame Martin.'

'Madame Martin. Right.'

'Ring at the door at the end of the corridor. If it's a woman with fair hair who answers it and if you recognize her, just make up an excuse. Say that you got the wrong floor or similar. If it's someone else, say that you want to speak to Madame Martin in person.'

'What do I do then?'

'Nothing. You come back here and confirm that she was the person you drove to Rue de Maubeuge this morning.'

'Right you are, inspector.'

When he had gone, in spite of himself, Maigret gave a little smile.

'With the first one, she'll start to worry. With the second, if all goes well, she'll start to panic. With the third, provided Torrence can get his hands on him . . .'

Good! Nothing could go wrong!

Then Torrence phoned:

'I think I've found him, chief. I've unearthed a driver who picked up a young woman answering to the description, at Gare du Nord, but he did not take her to Boulevard Richard-Lenoir. She asked to be dropped on the corner of Boulevard Beaumarchais and Rue du Chemin-Vert.'

'Send him to me here.'

'Trouble is, he's had a few.'

'It doesn't matter. Where are you now?'

'The depot at Barbès.'

'It won't take you too much out of your way, so call in at Gare du Nord. Go to the left-luggage office. Unfortunately, the man on duty won't be the same as the one who was there this morning. Ask if they've checked in a small, brand-new fibre case, which shouldn't be very heavy, and also who left it with them, between nine thirty and ten this morning. Make a note of the number of the ticket. They won't let you have the case without a warrant. But get the name and address of the clerk who was on the counter this morning.'

'What do I do after that?'

'Phone me. I'm waiting for your second taxi-driver. Since he's been drinking, write my address on a piece of paper so he doesn't get lost on the way.'

Madame Maigret had slipped away to her kitchen, where she was busy making the dinner, without daring to ask if Lucas would be eating with them.

Was Paul Martin still in the apartment opposite with his daughter?

Had Madame Martin tried to get rid of him?

When the doorbell rang, there was not one man on the landing but two, neither known to the other, who were exchanging amazed glances.

The first taxi-driver, already back from the apartment building opposite, found himself walking up Maigret's stairs at the same time as the man from the luggage shop.

'Did you recognize her?'

'Not only did I recognize her, but she recognized me too. She turned pale. She rushed inside and closed a door to a bedroom, then she asked me what I wanted.'

'What did you say?'

'That I had got the wrong floor. I could tell she didn't quite buy that and I decided not to give her time to make up her mind. When I got outside, I saw her looking down out of her window. She probably knows I came here.'

The man who sold suitcases had no idea what was going on. He was middle-aged, completely bald and had an unctuous manner. When the taxi-driver had gone, Maigret explained what was expected of him, and he expressed objections, repeating obstinately:

'You must understand that she is a customer. Betraying a customer's confidence is a very delicate matter.'

In the end, he decided to go, but as a precaution Maigret sent Lucas to follow him, in case he changed his mind on the way.

Less than ten minutes later they were back.

'May I point out I have acted only on your orders, that I was coerced and left with no choice.'

'Did you recognize her?'

'Will I be called to give evidence on oath?'

'It's more than likely.'

'That won't do my business any good. People who buy luggage at the last moment are sometimes people who would prefer it if their comings and goings were not aired in public.'

'If needs be, it might be enough if just the examining magistrate heard your statement.'

'In that case, it's definitely her. She's not wearing the same clothes, but I recognized her.'

'And did she recognize you?'

'The first thing she did was to ask who had sent me.'

'What was your answer?'

'I don't know exactly. I felt very awkward. I said I'd got the wrong door . . .'

'Did she offer you anything?'

'What do you mean? She didn't even ask me in to sit down. That would have been even more unpleasant.'

Whereas the taxi-driver had not asked for anything, the businessman, who was probably very comfortably off, insisted on being compensated for his time.

'All that remains now, Lucas, is to wait for the third one.'

Meanwhile, Madame Maigret was beginning to fret. From the door she made signs to her husband, discreetly she hoped, asking him to come to her in the kitchen, where she whispered:

'Are you sure that the father is still there, across the road?'

'Why?'

'I don't know. I don't understand exactly what you're up to. I'm thinking about the little girl and I feel a little frightened . . .'

Night had fallen some time before. Families had gone home. Not many windows remained dark in the building opposite, and the shadow of Madenoiselle Doncœur could still be made out in hers.

Maigret, still without collar and tie, finished getting dressed while he waited for the second taxi-driver. He called to Lucas:

'Help yourself. Are you hungry?'

'I'm brimful of sandwiches, chief. When we go out, there's only one thing I want: a glass of beer pulled straight from the barrel.'

The second driver arrived at 6.20. At 6.35, he came back from the other building. There was a louche glint in his eye.

'She's even more of an eyeful in a dressing gown than in a suit,' he said in a breathy voice. 'She made me go in and asked who had sent me. Since I didn't know what to say, I told her it was the director of the Folies-Bergère. She was furious. All the same, she's a fine figure of a woman. I don't know if you've seen her legs . . .'

It was difficult to get rid of him, and they managed it only after giving him a glass of sloe-gin, because he kept eying the bottle with obvious interest.

'What are you thinking of doing next, chief?'

Rarely had Lucas seen Maigret take so many precautions or prepare his move so carefully, as though he were going up against very strong opposition. Surely he was only dealing with a woman, an apparently unremarkable lower-middle-class one.

'Do you think she'll go on defending herself?'

'Yes, tooth and nail. And more than that, she'll do it with icy calm.'

'What are you waiting for?'

'Torrence's phone call.'

It came in on cue. It was all like a well-orchestrated score.

'The suitcase is here. It feels as if it's almost empty. As you thought, they won't give it to me without a warrant. As to the counter-clerk who was on duty this morning, he lives in the suburbs, out towards La Varenne-Saint-Hilaire.'

Anyone might have thought that, this time, there would be a hitch, or at least a delay. However, Torrence went on:

'But there's no need to go traipsing all the way out there.

After he finishes work for the day, he plays the cornet in a dance hall in Rue de Lappe.'

'Go and get him for me.'

'Do you want me to bring him to your apartment?'

Perhaps after all, Maigret also fancied a cool glass of beer.

'No, bring him to the building across the boulevard, third floor, Madame Martin's apartment. I'll be there.'

For this outing, he took his heavy overcoat from its peg and said to Lucas:

'Are you coming?'

Madame Maigret ran out after him to ask what time he would be back for dinner.

He hesitated and then smiled.

'The usual time!' he replied, which was not very helpful.

'Mind you take good care of that little girl.'

5.

At ten o'clock that night, they still had not obtained a positive result. Probably no one was asleep in the building, except Colette, who in the end had dropped off while her father continued to keep watch at her bedside in the dark.

At 7.30, Torrence had arrived, escorting the clerk from the left-luggage office, a musician in his spare time, who with as little hesitation as the others had declared:

'That's her all right! I can still see her now, putting the ticket not in her handbag but into her brown canvas shopping bag.'

They went to the kitchen and got the bag for him.

'That's the one. Or at any rate it's the same style and the same colour.'

It was very hot in the apartment. They all kept their voices down, as if by tacit agreement, because of the little girl who was sleeping in the next room. No one had eaten or even thought of eating. Before coming up, Maigret and Lucas had drunk two beers in a small bar on Boulevard Voltaire.

As for Torrence, after the musician had gone, Maigret had taken him out into the corridor and given him his orders in a whisper.

It seemed that there was only one place left in the

apartment that had not been thoroughly searched. Even the framed photographs of Martin's parents had been taken down to make sure that the ticket issued by the left-luggage office had not been slipped into the cardboard mount. The crockery which had been removed from the cupboard was in piles on the kitchen table, and even the food-safe had been completely emptied out.

Madame Martin still had on the pale blue dressing gown she had been wearing when the two men had arrived. She smoked one cigarette after another, and, together with the smoke from their pipes, there formed a dense cloud which coiled around the lights.

'You have the right to say nothing and refuse to answer any questions. Your husband is due to get in at eleven seventeen, and perhaps you will be more talkative when he gets here.'

'He doesn't know any more than I do.'

'But does he know as much as you?'

'There's nothing to know. I've told you everything.'

In fact she had opted to deny everything, all down the line. She had given way on just one thing. When they had brought up the subject of the apartment building in Rue Pernelle, she had admitted that her former employer had paid her a visit there at night, on two or three occasions, out of the blue. Even so, she maintained that there had never been any intimacy between them.

'In other words, they were purely business calls at one in the morning?'

'He'd just got off a train and often had large sums of money with him. I have already told you that sometimes he was involved in smuggling gold. I wasn't mixed up in that. You can't pin anything of that on me.'

'Did he have a large sum of money on him when he disappeared?'

'I don't know. He didn't always keep me informed about that side of his business.'

'But he did use to come to your room at night to talk to you about it?'

As to her movements that morning, she denied everything, despite all the evidence against her, claiming that she had never seen any of the men who had been sent to her before: the two taxi-drivers, the man from the suitcase shop and the clerk from the left-luggage office.

'To prove I really went and left a parcel at Gare du Nord, you'll need to find the ticket.'

He was more or less certain that they would not find it in the apartment, or even in Colette's room, which Maigret had searched before the little girl had gone off to sleep. He had even thought of the plaster which encased the child's leg and had not been renewed recently.

'Tomorrow,' she announced in a hard voice, 'I shall make a formal complaint. This is a trumped-up charge brought against me by the malice of a neighbour. I was right to be suspicious of her this morning when she absolutely insisted on dragging me to see you at home.'

She kept glancing anxiously at the alarm-clock on the mantelpiece and was obviously thinking about her husband's return. Yet, despite her impatience, no question succeeded in catching her out.

'Why not admit that the man who came here last night

didn't find anything under the floorboards because you'd changed the hiding place?'

'I don't even know if there ever was anything under the floor.'

'When you learned that he had been and had decided to reclaim what you were hiding, you thought of the left-luggage office, where your valuables would be safe.'

'I never went to Gare du Nord, and there are thousands of women with fair hair in Paris who answer to my description.'

'What have you done with the ticket? It's not here. I'm certain it's not in the apartment, but I think I know where we'll find it.'

'Aren't you the clever one!'

'Sit down at the table.'

He gave her a sheet of paper and a pen.

'Write!'

'What do you want me to write?'

'Your name and address.'

She obeyed after a moment's hesitation.

'Tonight, all the letters posted in letterboxes near here will be checked, and I'd bet there'll be one with your handwriting on which will be recognized. It is more than likely that you posted it to yourself.'

He told Lucas to go out and phone an inspector to arrange for the search to be carried out along these lines. In reality, he did not think he would get a result, but the threat had hit home.

'It's the classic move,' he barked.

It was the first time he had spoken to her in this way,

as he would have done at Quai des Orfèvres, and she reacted with a look of fury.

'You hate me, why don't you say it?'

'I will confess that my feelings for you are not of the warmest.'

They were now alone in the dining room, around which Maigret paced slowly while she remained seated at the table.

'And, if you're interested, I will also say that what shocks me most is not so much what you have done as your composure. I have had to deal with many people, both men and women. We've been here now, face to face, for three hours and it could be said that ever since this morning you have been under a tremendous strain. Yet you have not blinked once. Your husband will be here soon, and you will try to make out that you are the victim. But surely you must know that we will get to the truth sooner or later.'

'How will that get you any further forward? I haven't done anything wrong.'

'In that case, why hide anything? Why lie?'

She did not reply but sat there thinking. She wasn't losing her nerve, as happened in most cases. Her mind was working, looking for a way out, weighing up the pros and cons.

'I won't say anything,' she said eventually as she moved to an armchair and pulled her dressing gown down over her bare legs.

'As you wish.'

He settled comfortably into another armchair facing her.

'Are you intending to stay long in my apartment?'

'At least until your husband gets back.'

'Will you speak to him about Monsieur Lorilleux coming to see me at the hotel?'

'If it's absolutely necessary.'

'You're a brute! Jean doesn't know anything, he has nothing to do with this business.'

'Unfortunately he is your husband.'

When Lucas came back up, he found the two of them sitting opposite each other, not speaking, each furtively watching the other.

'Janvier will look after the letters, chief. I met Torrence downstairs. He told me our man was in the wine shop two buildings further along than yours.'

She immediately sprang to her feet.

'What man?'

To which Maigret, without moving, replied:

'The man who came here last night. I assume that, since he did not get what he came for, you were expecting he'd come back to see you. And this time, he might perhaps not be in quite the same frame of mind.'

She looked up fearfully at the clock. Only another twenty minutes, and the train from Bergerac would arrive in the station. If her husband got a taxi, she could count at most on having another forty minutes.

'Do you know who he is?'

'I have a good idea. I only have to go down to make sure. It's obviously Lorilleux, and he is anxious to be reunited with his property.'

'It's not his property.'

'Then let's just say that, right or wrong, he considers it to be his. He must be flat broke. He's already come to see you twice without getting what he wanted. Then he returned disguised as Father Christmas and is going to come back again. He will be very surprised to find you in our company, and I am convinced that he will be rather more forthcoming than you. Contrary to what people think, men talk more easily than women. Do you think he'll be armed?'

'I don't know.'

'In my opinion, he will be. He's tired of waiting. I have no idea what tale you've spun him but he doesn't believe it any more. Anyway, the man is liable to turn nasty. There's nobody more vicious than these quiet types when they put their minds to it.'

'Shut up!'

'Would you like us to go away and leave you two together?'

Among Maigret's scribbled notes is the entry:

'10.38 – she starts talking.'

But no written record was taken of that first statement. It consisted of broken phrases which she spat out waspishly, and Maigret, chipping in as often as the occasion arose, responded positively with what were perhaps shots in the dark, while she either stood her ground or just corrected him.

'What is it you want to know?'

'Is it money in the case that was left at the station?'

'Banknotes. A little under a million.'

'Who did it belong to? To Lorilleux?'

'It was no more Lorilleux's than mine.'

'To one of his customers then?'

'A man named Julien Boissy, who used to come to the shop often.'

'What became of him?'

'He's dead.'

'How did he die?'

'He was killed.'

'Who killed him?'

'Monsieur Lorilleux.'

'Why?'

'Because I had led him to believe that if he had a large sum of money I would go away with him.'

'Were you already married?'

'Yes.'

'Don't you love your husband?'

'I hate mediocrity. I've been poor all my life. All my life I've heard nothing else talked about but money and the need to tighten belts. All my life I've seen people around me counting the pennies and I've had to count them too.'

And she turned on Maigret as if he was responsible for her hard times.

'Would you have gone away with Lorilleux?'

'I don't know. Perhaps for a time.'

'Long enough to take his money off him?'

'I hate you!'

'How was the murder committed?'

'Monsieur Boissy was a regular visitor to the shop.'

'A collector of erotic books?'

'He was depraved, like the rest of them, just like Monsieur Lorilleux, like you probably. He was a widower and lived alone in a hotel, but he was very well-off and a miser with it. All rich men are misers.'

'But you aren't rich.'

'I would have been . . .'

'. . . if Lorilleux hadn't turned up again. How did Boissy die?'

'He was terrified of currency devaluations and wanted gold, like everybody else at that time. Monsieur Lorilleux smuggled gold. He used to go to Switzerland regularly to acquire more. He insisted on being paid in advance. One afternoon, Monsieur Boissy brought a large sum of money to the shop. I wasn't there. I'd gone out on an errand.'

'Did you go deliberately?'

'No.'

'Didn't you suspect what was about to happen?'

'No. Don't you try to put words into my mouth! You'd be wasting your time. But when I got back, Monsieur Lorilleux was busy putting the body into a large chest which he had bought for the purpose.'

'Did you blackmail him?'

'No.'

'How do you explain that he disappeared after handing over the money to you?'

'Because I made him afraid.'

'By threatening to go to the police?'

'No. I just told him the neighbours had been giving me odd looks, and that it would perhaps be more prudent to put the money in a safe place for a while. I told him about a plank in the floor of my apartment. I said it was easy to lift it and put it back again. He thought it would be for just a few days. Two days later, he asked me to cross the frontier into Belgium with him.'

'You refused?'

'I convinced him a man who I thought looked like a police inspector had stopped me in the street and asked me questions. This frightened him. I gave him a small part of the money and promised I would join him in Brussels as soon as the danger was over.'

'What did he do with Boissy's body?'

'He moved it to a small house he owned in the country, on the banks of the Marne, and there I imagine he buried it or threw it in the river. To transport it, he used a taxi. Afterwards, no one ever mentioned Boissy. No one was concerned about his disappearance.'

'So you managed to pack Lorilleux off to Belgium by himself?'

'It was easy.'

'And you were able to keep him at arm's length for five years?'

'I used to write to him poste restante saying that he was wanted and if his name was not mentioned in papers, it was because a trap was being set for him. I told him I was forever being questioned by the police. I even succeeded in making him go to South America.'

'And he came back two months ago?'

'About then. He'd had enough.'

'Hadn't you sent him any money?'

'Very little.'

'Why?'

She did not answer but looked at the clock.

'Are you going to take me away? What are you accusing me of? I haven't done anything. I didn't kill Boissy. I wasn't even there when he died. I never helped him hide the body.'

'There's no need to worry about what's going to happen to you. You kept the cash because all of your life you wanted to have money, not to spend, but so that you would feel rich and shielded from poverty.'

'That is entirely my business.'

'When Lorilleux turned up and asked you to help him, or to keep the promise you'd made to run away with him, you made the most of Colette's accident to claim that you couldn't get at the hiding place? Is that right? You tried once again to make him leave the country.'

'He's been staying in Paris, in hiding.'

She drew her lips back instinctively into a strange smile and almost as a reflex she muttered:

'The fool! He could have shouted his name from the rooftops, and no one would have noticed!'

'Maybe, but it did not stop him dreaming up the Father Christmas plan.'

'But the money wasn't under the floorboards any more. It was here, under his nose, in my needlework box. All he had to do was lift the lid.'

'Ten or twelve minutes from now, your husband will be here, and Lorilleux, who is now on the other side of the boulevard, probably knows it because he made inquiries. He learned that Martin was in Bergerac and will certainly have looked up the times of the trains. Most probably he is now plucking up the courage to come. I would be very surprised if he isn't armed. Do you want to wait for the pair of them to come?'

'Get me out of here. Give me a minute to put on a dress . . .'

'Where's the left-luggage ticket?'

'At the poste restante on Boulevard Beaumarchais.'

She went into her bedroom. She did not close the door and, with no trace of modesty, took off her dressing gown, sat on the edge of the bed to put her stockings on, then chose a woollen dress from her wardrobe.

At the last moment she grabbed a travel bag and into it roughly stuffed various toiletries and items of underwear.

'Let's go straight away.'

'What about your husband?'

'I don't given a damn about that fool!'

'And Colette?'

She did not answer, merely gave a shrug. Mademoiselle Doncœur's door moved as they passed. When they were downstairs, just as they were stepping out on to the pavement, she was suddenly afraid and cowered between the two men as she peered into the fog all around her.

'Take her to Quai des Orfèvres, Lucas. I'm staying here.'

There was no car in sight, and it was patently obvious that she was terrified at the thought of walking into the dark escorted only by the diminutive Lucas.

'No need to be afraid. Lorilleux is nowhere near here.'

'You lied!'

Maigret went back into the apartment building.

His conversation with Jean Martin lasted for two long

hours, and most of that time was spent in the presence of his brother.

When Maigret walked out of the building at around 1.30 in the morning, he left the two men talking together. There was light under Mademoiselle Doncœur's door, but she did not dare open it, doubtless because she was too embarrassed, and made do with hearing the sound of Maigret's parting footsteps.

He crossed the boulevard, went up to his apartment and found his wife asleep in the armchair by the dining-room table, on which his place had been set. She woke with a start.

'Are you by yourself?'

When he gave her a look of amused surprise, she added:

'Didn't you bring the little girl back with you?'

'Not tonight. She's asleep. Tomorrow morning, you can go and fetch her, but you must take care to be nice to Mademoiselle Doncœur.'

'Really?'

'I'll have two nurses go with you with a stretcher.'

'But that means . . . Are we going to . . .?'

'Hush now! . . . It can't be permanent, you know. Jean Martin might find someone else . . . Or perhaps his brother will revert to being a normal human being again and some day start up a home of his own . . .'

'So in a word, she won't be ours?'

'Not ours to keep, no. Just on loan. I thought it would be better than nothing and that you'd be happy.'

'Of course I'm happy . . . But . . . Even so . . .'

She sniffled, felt for a handkerchief, did not find one and covered her face in her apron.

Seven Small Crosses in a Notebook

1.

'Where I come from,' said Sommer, who was making the coffee on an electric ring, 'we all used to go to midnight mass, though the village was half an hour's walk from the farm. We were five boys. Winters were colder in those days, because I can remember going there and back on a sledge.'

Lecœur, sitting at his switchboard with its hundreds of small round sockets, had pushed his headphones off his ears so that he could follow the conversation.

'Which part of France was that?'

'Lorraine.'

'The winters weren't any colder in Lorraine forty years ago than they are now, but back then farmers didn't have cars. How many times did you really go to midnight mass by sledge?'

'I don't know.'

'Three times? Twice? Just the once, maybe? But it stuck in your mind because you were a kid at the time.'

'Anyway, when we got back, we'd find this huge black pudding, the like of which I've never seen since. And that's not something I imagined. We never found out how my mother made it or what she put in it that made it so different from all other kinds. My wife has tried. She asked my oldest sister, who said she knew Ma's recipe.'

He walked over to one of the tall, curtainless windows on the other side of which was nothing but darkness and scratched the pane with a fingernail.

'Look! There's frost on this window! And that's something else that reminds me of when I was a kid. In the mornings, before I could get washed, I used to have to break the ice on the water in the pitcher though it was inside, in my bedroom.'

'Because there was no central heating then,' Lecœur objected mildly.

There were three of them, three 'owls of the night shift' as they were known, and they had been shut up in the huge control room since eleven the previous night. Now it was six in the morning, and tiredness had set in. The debris of food littered the furniture, together with three or four empty bottles.

A bulb the size of an aspirin tablet lit up on one of the walls.

'Eighteenth arrondissement,' murmured Lecœur clamping his headphones back on his head. 'It's Croulebarbe.'

He selected a jack and pushed it into one of the sockets.

'Croulebarbe? Your police van just left. What's happened?'

'A uniformed officer just called in from Boulevard Masséna. A couple of drunks fighting.'

Lecœur carefully entered a small cross in a column of his notebook.

'What are you doing at your end?'

'There's only four of us in the station. Two are playing dominoes.'

'Have you had any black pudding?'

'No, why?'

'No reason. I'll hang up now. There's something going on in the sixteenth arrondissement.'

A huge street map of Paris had been painted on the wall facing him and the small bulbs which lit up on it each represented a police station. As soon as a station received an alert for any reason, its light flashed on. Lecœur pushed in the corresponding jack.

'Hello? Chaillot? Your van has just been called out . . .'

In each of Paris's twenty arrondissements, under the blue lamp outside every police station, one or more police vans always stood ready to respond whenever they were called out.

'Say again?'

'Veronal.'

A woman, more than likely. It was the third of the night, the second in the elegant suburb of Passy.

Lecœur entered a cross in a different column, while Mambret, at his desk, filled in official forms.

'Hello, Odéon? What's happening in your area? . . . Stolen car?'

This one was for Mambret, who took notes, picked up another phone and dictated a description of the car to Piedbœuf, the telegraph operator, whose voice they could hear droning away just above their heads. It was the forty-eighth description of stolen vehicles which Piedbœuf had sent out over the police radio since eleven o'clock.

For other people, Christmas Eve had a special flavour

to it. Hundreds of thousands of Parisians flocked to theatres and cinemas. Thousands of others had gone on shopping until it was very late in the large department stores, where flustered sales staff on weary legs rushed about in a nightmarish daze in front of their almost empty shelves.

Behind drawn curtains there were family reunions, turkeys roasting and black puddings no doubt made, like Sommer's, from a family recipe lovingly handed down from mother to daughter.

There were children sleeping fitfully and parents noiselessly arranging presents under the tree.

There were restaurants and nightclubs where the tables had all been booked up for the past week. On the Seine was moored the Salvation Army floating barge, where down-and-outs queued up, their nostrils filled with alluring aromas.

Sommer had a wife and children. Piedbœuf, the telegraphist above them, had become a father the week before.

If there had not been frost on the inside of the windows, they would not have known that it was cold outside, nor could they have said what shade of what colour that special night was. As far as they were concerned, it was the yellowish colour that filled their huge office opposite the Palais de Justice, which was part of the now empty buildings of the Préfecture de Police all around them. Not until the day after Christmas would people turn up again in hordes to apply for residence permits, driving licences or visas for passports and to make inquiries of all kinds.

In the courtyard below, police wagons stood ready to respond to urgent calls, and in them men dozed in their seats.

But there had been no emergencies. The small crosses in Lecœur's log were eloquent. He did not bother to count them. He knew that there were almost two hundred in the drunks' column.

Because on that night, obviously, some latitude was allowed. Uniformed officers tried to persuade revellers to go home without making trouble. They intervened only when drunks turned nasty and started smashing wine glasses or threatening law-abiding drinkers.

In various police stations, 200 men – and a handful of women – slept heavily on bare boards, behind bars.

Five stabbings, two at Porte d'Italie and three in the fringes of Montmartre – not the Montmartre of the night-clubs, but in the area of shacks made of old wooden chests and tarred felt where more than a hundred thousand North Africans live.

A few lost children – mostly found again soon after – among the crowds of worshippers at midnight mass.

'Hello, Chaillot? How's the woman who took Veronal doing?'

She wasn't dead. Her sort rarely die. They arrange things so that they don't. The gesture is enough.

'Talking of black pudding,' began Randon, who was smoking a large meerschaum pipe, 'reminds me . . .'

They never found out what it reminded him of. From the unlit staircase came the sound of uncertain foot-steps and a hand groping in the dark, and they saw the door knob turn. All three stared, surprised that anyone should think of dropping in on them like this at six in the morning.

'How are things?' the man said as he dropped his hat on a chair.

'What the devil are you doing here, Janvier!'

The newcomer was young, an inspector from the Murder Squad. The first thing he did was to stand by the radiator and warm his hands.

'I was getting fed up being all on my lonesome across the way. If the killer gets up to his tricks again, this is the place where I'll hear about it first.'

He had been on duty all night too, but on the opposite side of the street, in the offices of the Police Judiciaire.

'May I?' he asked, lifting the coffee pot. 'That wind is freezing.'

His ears were red, and he kept blinking.

'We won't know anything until eight this morning,' said Lecœur, 'probably later.'

He had been spending his nights here for fifteen years, sitting in front of the map with the flashing lights, manning his switchboard. He knew most of the uniformed men in Paris by name, or at any rate the ones on the night shift. He also knew all about their personal lives because when things were quiet and his little bulbs remained unlit for long stretches, they chatted over the airwaves.

'How are things with you?'

He also knew most police stations, though not all. He imagined the atmosphere of them and the men just in from their beat with their belts loosened and collars undone, making coffee exactly as they were doing here. But he had never actually met any of them. He would not have recognized them in the street. Nor had he ever set foot in any of the hospitals whose names were as familiar to him as the names of aunts and uncles were to other people.

'Hello! Bichat? How is that man with the knife wound they brought in twenty minutes ago? Dead?'

A small cross entered in the log. You could ask him difficult questions, such as: how many crimes are committed in Paris every year which have money as the motive?'

And he would answer without hesitating:

'Sixty-seven.'

How many murders are committed by foreigners?

'Forty-two.'

How many . . .?

He was in no sense proud of this. He was just meticulous: that was the top and bottom of it. It was his job. He wasn't required to enter little crosses in his little book, but it helped pass the time and it gave him as much satisfaction as collecting postage stamps.

He wasn't married. No one even knew where he lived, what he did after he left the office, where he went at night. Actually, it was hard to imagine him outside, in the street, like everyone else.

'For the important stuff,' he would say, 'you have to wait for people to be up and about, for the porter to bring up the mail, for the maids to start making breakfast and go and wake up their employers.'

There was no particular merit in knowing this, because that was always how it happened. Earlier in winter, later in summer. And today it would be even later, given the fact that most of the population would be sleeping off the effects of the previous evening's wine and champagne. There were still people in the streets, and restaurant doors kept opening to let out the last customers.

More stolen vehicles were reported. And also, probably, two or three drunks overcome by the cold.

'Hello? Saint-Gervais?'

His Paris was a Paris apart, whose principal sights were not the Eiffel Tower, the Opera and the Louvre, but dark, administrative buildings with a police van parked under a blue lamp and, leaning against its wall, the bicycles of the cycle-mounted police patrols.

'The chief,' said Janvier, 'is convinced that our man will make a move tonight. It's just the night for men like him. Celebrations get them worked up.'

No name was mentioned, because his name was not known. Nor could anyone speak of 'the man in the beige overcoat' or 'the man with the grey hat', because no one had ever seen him. Some newspapers had dubbed him 'Monsieur Dimanche' because three of his murders had been committed on a Sunday, but since those there had been a further five, which had occurred on other days at an average of one a week, though not according to any regular pattern.

'Was it because of him that you were put on duty tonight?'

It was also the reason why the level of night-time

surveillance had been stepped up throughout Paris, which for both uniformed men and inspectors meant overtime.

'When you do get your hands on him,' said Sommer, 'he'll turn out to be another loony.'

'A loony who goes round killing people,' sighed Janvier as he sipped his coffee. 'Hey! One of your little lights has come on.'

'Hello? Bercy? Your van has just been called out? . . . How? . . . Just a moment . . . Drowned?'

They watched as Lecœur hesitated over which column to use to add his cross. There was one for hangings and another for suicides who didn't own a gun and jumped out of windows instead. There were separate columns for those who drowned, or were shot, or . . .

'Listen a minute! Do you know what some idiot has just done on Pont d'Austerlitz? Who was talking just now about people with no brains? This one tied a stone to his ankles, climbed on to the parapet with a rope around his neck and then put a bullet in his brain!'

But there was a column for that too: 'Nerves'.

It was now the time when people who had not been making merry the night before were going to the first mass of the day, noses running and hands thrust deep into pockets, leaning into the wind which scoured the streets with a fine spray of ice. It was also the time of day when children began waking up, turned on the lights and scurried off with nothing on their feet and still in their night-clothes towards the tree of wonders.

'According to the pathologist, if our man really was a

lunatic, he would always kill in the same way, with a knife or gun or whatever.'

'What did he use last time?'

'A hammer.'

'And the time before?'

'A dagger.'

'What proof is there that it's the same man?'

'First, there's the fact that all eight murders were committed more or less one after the other. It would be surprising if eight new murderers had suddenly started operating in Paris.'

It was clear that Inspector Janvier had heard a great deal about the case over at the Police Judiciaire.

'But there's also the fact that all the murders seem to be similar. Each time, the victim is someone isolated; they may be young or old, but they are always isolated. People who live alone and have no family or friends.'

Sommer glanced at Lecœur, whom he could not forgive for being a bachelor and especially for not having children. He himself had five, and his wife was expecting their sixth.

'Sounds just like you, Lecœur! You'd better watch your step!'

'There's another link: the areas in which he operates. Not one of the murders has been committed in the affluent or even middle-class areas of the city.'

'But he's a thief too . . .'

'He steals, yes, but not much at any one time. Just small sums of money. Savings hidden under mattresses or wrapped in an old skirt. He doesn't ever break in, he never seems to carry much in the way of tools, like a burglar, and yet he never leaves any trace.'

A small light blinked on. Stolen car, taken from outside a restaurant on Place des Ternes not far from the Arc de Triomphe.

'The thing that most annoys those who suddenly discover they have no car is having to use the Métro to get home.'

Another hour or hour and a half and it would be the change of shift, except for Lecœur, who had agreed to fill in for a friend who had gone to spend Christmas with his family somewhere near Rouen.

It happened all the time. It had become so unremarkable that colleagues no longer hesitated before asking:

'Ah, Lecœur! Could you fill in for me tomorrow?'

At first, colleagues had used sob-stories: a sick mother or a funeral or a first communion. They would bring him a cake, some expensive charcuterie or a bottle of fine wine.

In reality, if he had been able to, Lecœur would have spent the twenty-four hours of every day in this large control room, sometimes catching up on his sleep on a camp bed, letting his dinner simmer on the electric ring. Oddly enough, though he was always as well turned-out as the others (and more so than some of them – Sommer, for example, whose trousers had rarely been pressed), there was always that sad look about him which identified him as a bachelor.

He wore spectacles with thick lenses better suited to a telescope, and they made his eyes look large and round, so that when he removed his glasses to clean them with the piece of chamois leather which he always kept in his pocket, it came as a surprise that the expression in his eyes was evasive, almost shy.

'Hello, Javel?'

It was one of the lights of the fifteenth arrondissement stations, just off Quai Javel, an area of factories, which had just flashed on.

'Has your van been called out?'

'We don't know what the trouble is yet. Someone's smashed the glass of an emergency phone in Rue Leblanc.'

'Didn't they say anything?'

'Not a peep out of them. The van's gone to check. I'll call you back.'

In Paris, hundreds of red police phone points are located along the kerbs of pavements. In an emergency, anyone can just break the glass to get straight through to the nearest police station. Had some passer-by accidentally smashed the glass of this one?

'Hello. Control? Our van has just got back. There was no one about. The area is quiet. We've got men patrolling the streets there.'

In the last column, for 'miscellaneous', Lecœur conscientiously entered a small cross.

'Any coffee left?' he asked.

'I'll make some more.'

The same bulb on the map lit up. Not ten minutes had elapsed since the first call.

'Javel? What have you got?'

'Another emergency glass smashed.'

'No one spoke?'

'Not a word. It'll be some card, someone who thinks that getting in our hair is a laugh. This time we'll try and collar him.'

'What's the location?'

'Pont Mirabeau.'

'Really? He moves quickly!'

For it was a fair distance between the two red emergency phones. But these calls did not yet warrant much attention. Three days earlier, someone had broken the glass of one and shouted defiantly:

'Death to all cops!'

Janvier, who had his feet up on one of the radiators, started to doze off and when he heard the voice of Lecœur speaking down the phone again, he half-opened his eyes, saw that one of the bulbs was lit up and asked dreamily:

'Him again?'

'Another glass vandalized on Avenue de Versailles, yes.'

'This is ridiculous!' he murmured and he settled back into his drowsiness.

It would be late before the new day broke, not before 7.30. At intervals the faint sound of bells could be heard, but it came from another universe. Down below, the hapless men in uniform must be freezing in their emergency police wagons.

'Talking of black pudding . . .'

'What black pudding?' asked Janvier who, half asleep and rosy-cheeked, looked like a small child.

'The black pudding that my mother . . .'

'Hello? You're not telling me that someone has smashed the glass of one of your emergency phone points? . . . Repeat that, please! . . . You don't say . . . He's already smashed two in the fifteenth arrondissement! . . . No, they haven't caught him . . . But whoever it is can certainly shift! . . . He crossed the Seine over Pont Mirabeau . . . It looks like he's heading for the centre of town . . . Yes, try it . . .'

That made another small cross and by 7.30, half an hour before the new shift came on duty, there were five in the column.

Mad or sane, the man was certainly moving fast. True, the temperature was not conducive to loitering. At one stage, he had appeared to be following the banks of the Seine. But he was not going in a straight line. He had made a detour around the wealthy streets of Auteuil and had smashed a glass in Rue La Fontaine.

'He's just five minutes away from the Bois de Boulogne,' said Lecœur. 'If that's where he's making for, we'll lose track of him.'

But the man doubled back, or very nearly, and returned to the embankment, smashing the glass of a phone in Rue Berton, a stone's thrown from Quai de Passy.

The first reports had come from the poor, working-class districts of Grenelle. For a change of scene the man had only to cross the Seine and he would find himself walking along spacious streets where there wouldn't be a soul about at that time of the morning. Everything would, of course, be closed. His footsteps would have sounded loud on roads hardened by frost.

Sixth call from him: he had gone around the Trocadéro and was now in Rue de Longchamp.

'Who does he think he is, Hansel?' murmured Mambret. 'He hasn't got any bits of bread or white pebbles, so he's using broken glass instead.'

There were other reports, one after the other, more stolen cars, a gunshot somewhere near Rue de Flandre, a wounded man who claimed he had no idea who had shot at him, although he had been seen drinking all night with another man.

'Right! Javel's calling in again. Hello, Javel! I imagine it's about your man who keeps smashing glass: he can't have had time to return to his starting point . . . What? . . . Yes, he's still at it. By now he must be somewhere around the Champs-Élysées . . . What? . . . One moment . . . Go ahead . . . Rue where??? . . . Michat? . . . The 't' is silent, right . . . Between Rue Lecourbe and Boulevard Félix-Faure . . . Yes . . . there's a railway viaduct near there . . . Yes . . . I see . . . Number 17 . . . Who made the call? . . . The concierge? . . . She was already up and about at that hour? . . . Keep the noise down, you lot! . . . No I'm not talking to you. It's Sommer, he's boring everybody stiff going on about black pudding . . .

'You were saying, the concierge . . . I see . . . A big apartment building . . . run down . . . seven floors . . . Got it . . .'

It was a neighbourhood of buildings which were not old but so badly constructed that as soon as people had moved into them they immediately looked seedy. They stood on areas of waste ground, and their grim, blank walls and gable-ends plastered with garish advertisements towered over suburban houses and occasional detached bungalows.

'You're saying she heard someone running down the stairs and the front door being slammed shut . . . Was it unlocked? . . . The concierge doesn't know how it happened? . . . On what floor? . . . The mezzanine, overlooking the courtyard . . . Go on . . . I see that the van from the eighth arrondissement has just been called out and I'd bet anything that it's about my glass-smasher . . . An old woman . . . Say again? . . . Madame Fayet? . . . Worked as a cleaning woman . . . Dead? . . . A blunt instrument . . . Is the doctor there? . . . Are you sure she's dead? . . . Her savings were taken? . . . I only ask because I assume she had savings . . . All right . . . Ring me back . . . Or else I'll ring you . . .'

He turned to the sleeping inspector.

'Janvier! Hey! Janvier! I think this one is for you.'

'Who? What is it?'

'The killer.'

'Where?'

'Javel. I've written the address on this piece of paper. This time he's killed an elderly cleaning woman, a Madame Fayet.'

Janvier got into his overcoat, looked round for his hat and swallowed the last of the coffee left in his cup.

'Who from the fifteenth arrondissement has been put on the case?'

'Gonesse.'

'Better let the Police Judiciaire know that's where I'll be.'

A moment later, Lecœur was adding a small cross in

his log, the seventh, in the last column. The glass of an emergency police phone had been shattered in Avenue d'Iéna, 150 metres from the Arc de Triomphe.

'Among the fragments of broken glass they found a handkerchief with traces of blood on it. A child's handkerchief.'

'Any initials on it?'

'No. It's a blue-checked handkerchief and none too clean. Whoever it was must have wrapped it around their fist to break the glass.'

The sound of footsteps came from the staircase. It was the new shift, the day men. They were clean-shaven and, judging by their pink tightly stretched skin, they had washed in cold water before heading off into the icy wind.

'Well, did you boys live it up last night?'

Sommer closed the small metal box in which he had brought his own food. Only Lecœur did not move, because he was staying put and would become part of this new replacement team too.

Portly Godin was already getting into the linen overall he wore for work. The moment he came in he'd put water on to boil to make grog. All winter he had been dogged by the same cold which he treated – or cultivated – with regular doses of rum and hot water.

'Hello? Yes . . . No, I'm not going off duty . . . I'm standing in for Potier, who has gone away to see his family . . . Anyway . . . Yes, I've got a personal interest in it . . . Janvier has left, but I'll pass the message on to the Police Judiciaire . . . Disabled? . . . Who's disabled?'

You always need patience at the outset to grasp what's going on, because colleagues tell you about the case they are investigating as if everybody was fully in the picture.

'The house at the back, yes . . . so it's not actually in Rue Michat . . . Rue what? . . . Rue Vasco-de-Gama? . . . That's right, I know it . . . Small house with a garden and a wrought-iron gate . . . I didn't know he was an invalid . . . Sure . . . He hardly ever sleeps . . . Some kid who climbed up the drainpipe? . . . How old? . . . He doesn't know? . . . That's true, it was dark . . . How does he know it was just a kid? . . . Listen, I'd appreciate it if you could ring me back . . . You're going off duty too? . . . Who is replacing you? . . . Jules? . . . The one who . . . Yes . . . Right . . . Tell him hello from me and ask him to give me a call.'

'What's going on?' asked one of the new men.

'An old woman who got murdered in Javel.'

'By who?'

'Some sort of invalid who lives in the house behind her block claims he saw a young kid climbing up the wall towards her window.'

'Did this kid kill her?'

'Well, we know for a fact that a child's handkerchief was found near an emergency police phone.'

They listened with only half an ear. The room was still lit, but raw morning light was filtering through windows covered with frost patterns. Again, one of the men went and scratched the glass and made it squeak. It's an instinctive thing, maybe a childhood memory, like Sommer's black pudding.

The night staff had all gone. Their replacements were getting organized, settling in for the day, perusing reports.

Stolen car, La Bruyère Square.

Lecœur pored over his seven small crosses, concentrating hard, then he got up and stood in front of the large wall map.

'Are you committing your street map to memory?'

'I know it already. But there's something that strikes me. Within the space of about an hour and a half, the glass of seven police phones has been broken. Now, it seems to me that whoever is playing this little game was not only not walking in a straight line, not following a specific route to get from one point to another, but has been moving in fairly frequent zigzags.'

'Perhaps he doesn't know Paris?'

'Or maybe he knows it too well. Not once has he gone anywhere near a police station, though he would have passed a number on his way if he had chosen the shortest route. And at which intersections and roundabouts would he have been likely to bump into a policeman?'

He pointed at them with one finger.

'He didn't pass any of them either. He made detours around them. The only risk he ran was when he crossed over Pont Mirabeau, but he would have run the same risk wherever he crossed the Seine.'

'He's probably had too much to drink,' joked Godin as he blew on his rum and sipped it slowly.

'What I'm wondering is why he has stopped smashing the glass on phones.'

'He has probably reached home.'

'The chances that a man who happens to be in the Javel district at six in the morning will live anywhere near the Arc de Triomphe are pretty slim.'

'Why get so worked up about it?'

'It scares me.'

'You're kidding!'

It really was the most surprising thing to see Lecœur looking worried, because to him the most eventful nights in Paris were invariably reduced to a few small crosses in a logbook.

'Hello, Javel! . . . Is that Jules? . . . It's Lecœur . . . Listen . . . The house of the invalid is behind that apartment block in Rue Michat . . . Right . . . But next to it there's another block, a red-brick building, with a grocery store on the ground floor . . . Yes . . . Has anything been going on there? . . . Has the concierge reported anything? . . . I don't know . . . No, I have no information . . . It might be an idea to go over there and ask her, yes.'

He suddenly felt hot. He stubbed out a cigarette that he had barely started.

'Hello? Les Ternes? . . . I don't suppose you've had any calls from emergency phones in your area? . . . None at all? Only drunks? Thanks. But since you're there . . . Have your mounted patrol boys gone out on their bikes already? . . . Just setting off? Right, would you ask them to keep an eye open for a kid? . . . A youngster who'll be looking tired and have a bleeding right hand . . . No, it's not a missing person . . . I'll explain another time . . .'

He did not take his eyes off the wall map, where no lights flashed on for a good ten minutes. And when one did it was for an accidental death by gas inhalation in the eighteenth arrondissement, on the heights of Montmartre.

In all the cold streets of Paris, there were now only the black-garbed figures of the faithful returning chilled to the bone from early-morning mass.

2.

One of the clearest impressions André Lecœur retained from his childhood was that of changelessness. In those days, his world was a large kitchen in Orléans, on the edge of town. He must have spent all his winters there and all his summers too, but in his mind's eye it was almost invariably flooded with sunlight, with the door open and across it a slatted gate which his father had knocked together one Sunday to stop him going out by himself into the garden, where hens clucked and rabbits spent all day munching in their chicken-wire cages.

At 8.30, his father would ride off on his bike to the gasworks on the other side of town, where he worked. His mother would do the housework, always in the same order, going upstairs to the bedrooms, where she draped the mattresses over the window-sills.

In next to no time, the bell rung by the grocery man as he pushed his cart through the streets would indicate that it was ten o'clock. Twice a week, at eleven, the doctor with the beard would come to see his little brother, who was always ill and whose room he was not allowed to enter.

That was all. Nothing else happened. He hardly had time to play or drink his glass of milk before his father was home for lunch.

By then, his father had dug trenches in several parts of town, where he had met lots of people. As they ate, he talked about them, and time had almost stood still. And then during the afternoon (perhaps his nap had helped), it had flown by even more quickly.

'I've hardly got through the housework,' his mother would sigh, 'before it's time to start making the dinner.'

It was rather like that here, in this large room in the central telephone exchange, where the air itself never moved, and men grew sluggish until bells ringing and voices speaking seemed to come through a thin veil of sleep.

A few bulbs lighting up on the wall map, a few small crosses – a car had just been hit by a bus in Rue de Clignancourt – and already the Javel police station was calling back.

This time it was not Jules. It was Inspector Gonesse, the officer who had been to the scene of the crime. They had had plenty of time to contact him and fill him in about the house in Rue Vasco-de-Gama. He had gone out there and had come back very excited.

'Is that you, Lecœur?'

There was something peculiar about his voice, perhaps bad temper or suspicion.

'Look, how is it you came up with that particular house? Did you know Madame Fayet?'

'I never set eyes on her, but I know her.'

What was now happening on this Christmas morning was something that André Lecœur had been expecting for ten years. More specifically, whenever he let his eye wander over the map of Paris where the lights blinked on, he would sometimes think:

'One of these days, it is written that the report will be about someone I know.'

There was the odd occasion when something did happen in his neighbourhood, near his street but never quite in it. Like a storm, the prospect came nearer then retreated without breaking over the exact spot where he lived.

But this time, it had happened.

'Have you questioned the concierge?' he said. 'Was she up?'

He pictured the noncommittal expression on the face of Inspector Gonesse at the other end of the line and went on:

'Is the boy at home?'

Gonesse growled:

'You mean you know him too?'

'He's my nephew. Didn't anyone tell you his name is Lecœur, François Lecœur?'

'They told me.'

'And?'

'He's not at home.'

'What about his father?'

'He got home this morning just after seven.'

'As he always does, I know. He works nights, like me.'

'The concierge heard him going up to his apartment. It's on the third floor overlooking the courtyard.'

'I know.'

'He came back down almost straight away and knocked on the door of her lodge. He seemed very upset. To quote the concierge, he looked "beside himself".'

'Has the boy disappeared?'

'Yes. The father wanted to know if anyone had seen him go out and at what time. The concierge didn't know. Then he asked if a telegram had been delivered yesterday evening or early this morning.'

'Was there a telegram?'

'No. Can you make anything of it? Don't you think, since you're family and know the background, that it would be better if you came out here yourself?'

'There's no point. Where is Janvier?'

'In old Madame Fayet's bedroom. The team from Criminal Records have just arrived and have already started work. The first thing they turned up was a child's fingerprints on the door knob. Why don't you come round?'

Lecœur replied weakly:

'There's no one here to replace me.'

That was true, though if pushed, by phoning around, he could have found a colleague prepared to spend an hour or two at the main switchboard. But the fact was, he didn't want to be on the spot; it wouldn't have been helpful.

'Listen, Gonesse, I've got to find that kid, do you understand? Half an hour ago he was probably wandering about near the Arc de Triomphe. Tell Janvier I'm staying here, also that it's likely that old Madame Fayet had a lot of money hidden in her apartment.'

With feverish haste, he removed the jack from its socket and rang round all the various police stations in the eighth arrondissement.

'Keep your eyes peeled for a kid of about ten or eleven,

clothes nothing unusual, and pay particular attention to emergency phone points.'

His two colleagues eyed him with curiosity.

'Do you reckon the kid did it?'

He did not bother to give them an answer. He was calling the central switchboard upstairs.

'Justin! This is a surprise! So it's you on duty? . . . Look, would you call all radio cars and ask them to look out for a youngster of about ten who is wandering around somewhere near the Arc de Triomphe? . . . No I don't know which direction he's going in. He seems to be avoiding streets where there are police stations and the main intersections where he might come across a uniformed officer.'

He knew the apartment where his brother lived in Rue Vasco-de-Gama, two dark rooms and a tiny kitchen, where the boy was left on his own every night while his father went out to work. From the windows, the back of the apartment building in Rue Michat was plainly visible, along with washing hanging out to dry, potted geraniums plus, behind the windowpanes, many of which had no curtains, glimpses of the many and varied aspects of human existence.

But it was also true that those panes would also be obscured by frost. The thought struck him and he filed it away in a corner of his memory, for he had a feeling it might well turn out to be important later.

'So you think it's a boy who is vandalizing the glass of those emergency phones?'

'They found a child's handkerchief,' he said curtly.

And he sat there in a sort of trance, feeling numbed and wondering in which socket he should insert his jack.

Outside, people seemed to be moving at amazing speeds. In the time it took Lecœur to respond to a call, the doctor had arrived at the crime scene, followed by the deputy public prosecutor and an examining magistrate who had to be dragged out of bed.

What was the point of his going out there, since from where he was he could visualize the streets and the buildings – including the railway viaduct, which drew a thick black line across the entire landscape – as clearly as those who were on the spot could actually see them?

Only people with not much money lived in that neighbourhood, the young dreaming of getting out of there one day, the not so young who were beginning to lose hope, the even less young, the almost old and lastly the really old who struggled to make the best of the hand dealt them by fate.

He rang Javel once more.

'Is Inspector Gonesse still there?'

'He's writing up his report. Shall I call him?'

'Please . . . Hello! Gonesse? . . . It's Lecœur. Sorry to bother you. Have you been to my brother's apartment? . . . Good! Had the boy's bed been slept in? . . . That goes some way to putting my mind at rest . . . No, wait. Were there any bags of shopping? . . . Yes, shopping . . . What? A chicken, black pudding, Saint-Honoré cheese and . . . I didn't understand that last part . . . A small radio? . . . Still in its box? . . . Obviously . . . Is Janvier still out that way? . . . He has already phoned in to the Police Judiciaire? . . . Thanks . . .'

He was very surprised to see that it was already 9.30. It was no use now looking at the Arc de Triomphe sector on the map of Paris. If the boy had gone on walking at the same rate, he'd had enough time to get as far as any one of the capital's suburbs.

'Hello? Police Judiciaire? Is Inspector Saillard in his office?'

He too must have been dragged out of his warm apartment by Janvier's phone call. How many people were going to have their Christmas ruined by this business?

'I'm sorry to ring you, inspector. It's about the Lecœur boy.'

'Do you know something? Is he a relative of yours?'

'He's my brother's son. He was probably the one responsible for breaking the glass in the seven emergency phones. I don't know if anyone has had time to tell you that we lost track of him after the Arc de Triomphe. I would like to ask your permission to put out a general call.'

'Can you come round and see me here?'

'There's no one here on hand to replace me.'

'Put out that call. I'm on my way.'

Lecœur remained calm, but his hand shook a little as it hovered over the jacks.

'Is that you, Justin? A call to all cars. Give a description of the boy. I don't know what he's wearing but it's probably his khaki jacket made out of an American Army battle-dress. He's tall for his age and on the skinny side . . . No, he doesn't wear a cap. He is always bare-headed, with hair hanging down over his forehead. Perhaps it would also be an idea to give a description of his father. I find that harder. You know me, don't you? Well, we're alike, only he's a paler version of me. He gives the impression of being shy and doesn't look very strong. He's the sort of man who doesn't occupy the middle of the pavement but sidles along the walls of buildings. He walks slightly slantwise because he got a bullet in the foot in the war . . . No, I don't have any idea of where they might be making for. I don't believe they are together. But it's more than probable that the boy is in danger . . . Why? It would take too long to explain. Put out the call. Let me know if there's anything new . . .'

The phone call had taken so long that by the time it had finished Inspector Saillard had arrived. He had had ample time to leave the building on Quai des Orfèvres, cross the road and walk through the empty corridors of the Préfecture of Police. He was impressive to look at and wore an enormous overcoat. By way of a general greeting to all present, he just touched the brim of his hat. He pulled up a chair as if it were as light as a feather and sat down astride it. Finally, looking straight at Lecœur, he asked:

'Anything on the boy?'

'I'm wondering why he has stopped calling us.'

'Calling?'

'Why, if not to let us know where he was, would he have broken the glass of those emergency phones?'

'And why, after going to the trouble of breaking them, did he not say anything down the phone?'

'Maybe he was being followed? Or perhaps he was following someone?'

'I've thought about that. Listen, Lecœur, does your brother have money troubles?'

'He's not well off, yes.'

'Just not well off?'

'He lost his job three months ago.'

'What job?'

'He was a linotypist on *La Presse* in Rue du Croissant, where he worked nights. He has always worked nights. You could say it runs in the family.'

'Why did he lose his job?'

'Probably for falling out with someone.'

'Was that a habit of his?'

An incoming call interrupted them. It was from the eighteenth arrondissement, where they had just picked up a kid in the street at the corner of Rue Lepic. He was selling sprigs of holly, a Polish boy who did not speak a word of French.

'You asked me if he was in the habit of falling out with people? I don't really know what to say. My brother has been ill for most of his life. When we were young, he spent nearly all his time in his room, by himself, reading. He has read tons of books. But he never went to school regularly.'

'Is he married?'

'His wife died after they'd been married for two years and he was left alone with a ten-month-old baby.'

'Did he bring the boy up himself?'

'Yes I can still see him giving him his bath, changing him, making his bottles . . .'

'That doesn't explain why he got into arguments.'

True, but words clearly did not have the same meaning in the inspector's large head as they did in Lecœur's.

'Was he embittered?'

'Not especially. He was used to it.'

'Used to what?'

'Used to not having a life like other people's. Perhaps Olivier – that's my brother's name – isn't overly bright. Maybe he knows too much about some subjects from the books he has read, and not enough about people.'

'Do you think he's capable of killing old Madame Fayet?'

The inspector drew on his pipe. Above them, the telegraph operator could be heard walking around. The two other men in the room pretended they weren't listening.

'She was his mother-in-law,' Lecœur said quietly. 'You'd have found out for yourself sooner or later.'

'Didn't he get on with her?'

'She hated him.'

'Why?'

'Because she accused him of having been the ruination of her daughter. There had been an argument about an operation which was not carried out in time. It wasn't my brother's fault but the hospital's which had refused to admit her because the paperwork wasn't in order. Even so, the old girl always blamed my brother.'

'Didn't they have anything to do with each other?'

'I dare say they might have bumped into each other in the street because they lived in the same neighbourhood.'

'Did the boy know?'

'That old Madame Fayet was his grandmother? I don't think so.'

'His father didn't tell him?'

Lecœur's eyes never strayed from the map with its small bulbs, but it was a slow time of day, and they rarely came on, and when they did now it was almost certainly to report traffic accidents. There was also a case of pickpocketing on the Métro and a theft of luggage at Gare de l'Est.

But there was no news of the boy. Yet the streets of Paris remained half deserted. In working-class areas, children tried out their new toys on the pavements, but most houses stayed closed, and the warmth inside made their windows steam up. The shops had their blinds down, and there were just a handful of regulars in the small bars.

The only sounds were those of bells ringing out in all directions high over the roofs. Families dressed in their Sunday best entered churches, from which escaped the low rumble of great organs.

'Excuse me for a moment, inspector. I'm still thinking about the boy. It's obvious it's harder for him now to break the glass on any more phones without drawing attention to himself. But would it be an idea to check out the churches? He wouldn't go unnoticed in a bar or café, whereas in a church . . .'

He called up Justin again.

'Let's try the churches! Ask them to keep a lookout in churches. And stations. I hadn't thought about the stations either.'

He took off his glasses and his eyelids looked very red, perhaps because he had not slept.

'Hello! . . . Central exchange, yes . . . What? . . . Yes, the inspector is here.'

He passed an earpiece to Saillard.

'It's Janvier. He wants a word.'

Outside the wind was still blowing from the north, and the daylight was uniformly cool and hard with, however, behind the massed cloud, a hint of yellow, which was like a promise of sunshine.

As the inspector hung up, he growled:

'According to Dr Paul, the murder was committed between five and six thirty this morning. The old lady was not killed by the first blow. She must have been in bed when she heard a sound. She got up and confronted the intruder who she apparently hit with a shoe.'

'Has the murder weapon been found?'

'No. They think it was a length of lead pipe or a tool with a rounded face, a hammer perhaps.'

'Have they found the money?'

'They've got her purse. It only had a few low-denomination notes and her identity card in it. By the way, Lecœur, did you know that the old girl was a loan-shark?'

'I did.'

'Didn't you tell me a moment ago that your brother lost his job about three months ago?'

'That's correct.'

'The concierge didn't know.'

'Nor did his son. It was on the boy's account that he didn't say anything about it.'

The inspector crossed and uncrossed his legs, feeling very ill at ease. He looked around at the two other men, who could not have helped hearing. Then he stared at Lecœur as though he didn't know what to make of it all.

'Do you realize,' he began, 'what this . . .?'

'I do.'

'Had you thought about it?'

'No.'

'Because he's your brother?'

'No.'

'How long is it since the murderer first went on the rampage? Nine weeks, isn't it?'

Unhurriedly, Lecœur checked in his little notebook and searched for a cross in one column.

'Nine and a half weeks. The first murder was in the Épinettes district on the other side of Paris.'

'You just said your brother didn't tell his son that he was unemployed. So he went on leaving home and coming back at the same times? Why would he do that?'

'So as not to lose face.'

'What do you mean?'

'It's hard to explain. He's not like most fathers. He has brought the kid up entirely by himself. The pair of them live together. They're like an old married couple, if you take my meaning. During the day, my brother prepares the meals and does the housework. He puts his son to bed before going out and wakes him up when he gets back . . .'

'That doesn't explain . . .'

'Do you think that a man like that would want, in the eyes of his son, to look like a failure who finds all doors closed against him because he is unable to fit in?'

'And what did he do during all those nights over these last months?'

'He got a job for two weeks as a night watchman in a

factory out at Billancourt. He was just filling in for someone else. Most of the time he washed cars in garages. If he couldn't find anything better, he'd work as a porter toting vegetables at Les Halles. When he had an attack . . .'

'Attack of what?'

'Asthma. He had them from time to time . . . He would go and lie down in a station waiting room somewhere . . . Once, he spent the night here chatting with me . . .'

'What if the kid saw his father in old Madame Fayet's apartment early this morning?'

'The windows would have been iced up.'

'Not if the window was left slightly open. Even in winter, a lot of people sleep with the window open.'

'My brother doesn't. He feels the cold, and they're too poor to waste expensive heat.'

'Let's say the boy could have scraped the ice off with his fingernails. When I was small, I . . .'

'Me too. We need to know if Madame Fayet's window was open.'

'Her window was open and the light was on.'

'I wonder where François is now.'

'Is that the kid's name?'

He found it surprising, and rather unsettling, to see that Lecœur was thinking only of the child. It made him feel almost even more uncomfortable to hear him talk calmly about his brother in ways that did him no favours.

'When he got back this morning, he was carrying a number of carrier bags. Do you have any thoughts about that?'

'It's Christmas.'

'He must have had money to buy a chicken, cakes and a radio. Has he been round lately asking you for a loan?'

'Not for a month. I'm sorry he hasn't, because I would have told him not to buy a radio for François. I've got one for him, it's here in the staff cloakroom. I was intending to give it to him today after I finished work.'

'Would Madame Fayet have agreed to lend her son-in-law money?'

'It's unlikely. She was an odd woman. She must have had enough money to live on and yet she went on cleaning houses from morning till night. It wasn't unusual for her to lend money at high rates of interest to the people she worked for. Everyone in the neighbourhood knew. They went to her when they were a bit short at the end of the month.'

The inspector got to his feet, still feeling uneasy.

'I'm going down there to have a look round,' he said.

'To the old woman's apartment?'

'To her place and Rue Vasco-de-Gama both. If there are any developments at this end, give me a call.'

'Neither of the two buildings has a phone. I'll contact the police station and get to you that way.'

The inspector was on his way down the stairs with the door closed behind him when the phone rang. None of the lamps had blinked on. It was a call from Gare d'Austerlitz.

'Lecœur? Special inspector here. We've got your man.'

'What man?'

'The one whose description was circulated. His name is Lecœur, same as you, Olivier Lecœur. I checked his identity card.'

'Just a moment.'

He ran to the door, hurried down the stairs and it was only when he reached the courtyard with the parked police vans that he managed to catch Saillard just as he was getting into one of the Préfecture's small saloon cars.

'I've got Gare d'Austerlitz on the phone. They've found my brother.'

The inspector, a big, burly man, walked back up the stairs, breathing heavily. He picked up the receiver himself.

'Hello? . . . Where was he? . . . What was he doing? . . . What's his story? . . . I didn't catch . . . No, don't bother to interview him now . . . Are you sure he doesn't know? . . . Keep watching the station . . . It's very likely . . . As for our man, send him to me as soon as you can . . .'

He glanced up at Lecœur and hesitated.

'Under escort, yes. That'll be safest.'

He took a moment to fill his pipe and lit it before explaining, which he did as though he were speaking to no one in particular:

'They got him after he'd been roaming around the waiting rooms and platforms for an hour. It seems he's in a bit of a state. He said something about a message from his son. He's there because he's been waiting for the son to meet him there.'

'Did they tell him the old woman is dead?'

'Yes. It seems the news terrified him. They're bringing him in.'

He added uncertainly:

'I thought it best if he came here. Given the fact that you are family, I didn't want you to think . . .'

'Thank you.'

Lecœur had now been in the same room, sitting on the same chair, since eleven the night before, and it was just like when he was a boy in his mother's kitchen. Nothing moved around him. Little lights went on, he inserted jacks into sockets, time passed seamlessly without anyone noticing, and yet outside, Paris had seen in another Christmas, thousands of people had attended midnight mass; others had celebrated noisily in restaurants; drunks had spent the night in the cells of the Préfecture and come round under the eye of a custody officer; later, children had rushed to trees ablaze with lights.

What had his brother Olivier been doing during all that time? An old woman was dead, and before the new day had dawned a young boy had walked until he was gasping for breath through deserted streets and smashed the glass of several emergency police phones with his fist wrapped in a handkerchief.

What had Olivier, apprehensive and tense, been waiting for in the overheated waiting rooms and on the draughty platforms of Gare d'Austerlitz?

Less than ten minutes went by, just enough time for Godin, whose nose was now streaming in earnest, to make himself another grog.

'Would you like one, inspector?'

'No thanks.'

An embarrassed Saillard whispered to Lecœur:

'Would you like us to go into another room to inter-view him?'

But Lecœur had no intention of abandoning his wink-ing lights and his phone jacks which connected him with every part of Paris. There was a sound of footsteps coming up the stairs. Two officers, one on each side, escorted Olivier, whom, however, they had not handcuffed.

He looked like a bad photograph of André himself which had grown fuzzy with age. His eyes immediately settled on his brother.

'Where's François?'

'We don't know yet. We're looking.'

'Where?'

Lecœur could only gesture to the map and the innu-merable little holes in his switchboard.

'Everywhere.'

The two inspectors had already been sent away when Saillard said:

'Sit down. Did they tell you that old Madame Fayet is dead?'

Olivier did not wear spectacles, but he had the same pale, evasive eyes as his brother when he removed his glasses, so that he always gave the impression that he'd been crying. He looked for a moment at the inspector, to whom he seemed to attach no importance.

'He left me a note . . .' he said as he searched through the pockets of his old gaberdine. 'Do you understand what's going on, André?'

Eventually he produced a scrap of paper torn from a school exercise book. The handwriting was not very even.

The boy was very likely not one of the best pupils in his class. He had used an indelible pencil and had licked the end of it so that he now probably had a stain on his lips.

> Uncle Gideon is coming this morning, arriving at Gare
> d'Austerlitz. Meet us there.
> Love, Bott.

Without saying a word, André Lecœur handed the paper to the inspector, who turned it over several times between his fingers.

'Why Bott?'

'It's what I call him when we're by ourselves. Not in front of other people, because that would make him feel awkward. It's short for bottle and goes back to when I used to feed him with a bottle.'

He spoke in a neutral voice, with no accent, and probably without seeing anything around him except a kind of fog in which vague shapes moved to and fro.

'Who is Uncle Gideon?'

'There's no such person.'

Was he not aware that he was talking to the head of the Murder Squad, who was personally conducting a criminal investigation?

His brother explained:

'More accurately, someone who no longer exists. He was one of our mother's brothers. His name was Gideon. He went to America when he was very young.'

Olivier gave him a look which seemed to say:

'Why are you going on about that?'

'In the family, we got into the habit of saying for a joke: "One day Uncle Gideon will leave us a fortune." '

'Was he rich?'

'We had no idea. We never heard from him, just a post-card every New Year signed "Gideon".'

'Is he dead?'

'Yes, when Bott was four.'

'Do you think this is helping, André?' said Olivier.

'We're looking. Leave this to me. My brother has carried on the family tradition by telling his son about Uncle Gideon. He turned into a kind of character from a legend. Every day, before he went to sleep, the boy would ask for a story about Uncle Gideon, who had all sorts of made-up adventures. Naturally, he was fabulously rich and when he returned . . .'

'I think I understand. And he really is dead?'

'Died in hospital, in Cleveland, where he washed dishes in a restaurant. We never told the boy. We just carried on with the story.'

'Did he believe it?'

The boy's father intervened timidly. He came pretty close to putting his hand up, the way pupils do in class.

'My brother reckons he didn't,' he said, 'that François had guessed the truth, that it was only a game. But I think the opposite, I'm almost certain he still believed it. When other kids told him that there is no Father Christmas, he went on denying it for two years.'

As he talked about his son, he grew animated and became a quite different person.

'I can't understand why he should have written me that

note. I asked the concierge if a telegram had arrived. For a moment I thought André was having us on. Why on earth would François go out at six in the morning leaving a note saying I should rush off to Gare d'Austerlitz? I went there half out of my mind with worry. I looked everywhere. I kept expecting to see him arrive. Tell me, André, are you sure you . . .?'

But André was keeping an eye on the map on the wall and his switchboard. Every disaster, every accident that happened in Paris invariably ended up there.

'They haven't found him,' said Lecœur. 'They're still looking. At eight o'clock he was somewhere in the region of the Arc de Triomphe.'

'How do you know? Was he seen?'

'It's hard to explain. All along the route from your place to the Arc de Triomphe, someone kept breaking the glass on emergency police phones. A blue-checked child's handkerchief was found just by the last one.'

'He's got blue-checked handkerchiefs.'

'There's been nothing since eight o'clock.'

'In that case I've got to get back to the railway station at once. He's bound to go there because that's where he arranged for us to meet.'

He was astonished by the sudden silence which descended all around him. He looked at each of them in turn, his surprise changing to alarm.

'What is it?'

His brother averted his eyes. The inspector coughed and after a moment said uncertainly:

'Did you go and see your mother-in-law last night?'

Was it perhaps true, as his brother had intimated, that the way Olivier's mind worked was not entirely normal? The words took a long time to reach his brain. But it was more or less possible to read the slow workings of his thoughts in his face.

He stopped looking at the inspector and turned to his brother, his face suddenly flushed and his eyes very bright.

'André!' he cried. 'Surely you haven't dared . . .?'

His mood changed abruptly, he leaned forwards on the edge of his chair, took his head in both hands and started to sob noisily.

3.

Inspector Saillard glanced up at André Lecœur. He was surprised to see how calm he was and may even have been tempted to take exception to what must have seemed his indifference. Was it perhaps because Saillard did not have a brother? Lecœur had had experience of a sibling since early childhood. He had seen him pass through crises similar to this one when he was a boy, and in the circumstances he was almost relieved because it might all have been a lot worse: instead of tears, demoralized resignation and his special brand of dazed inertia, they might have had to contend with an Olivier who was angry, vociferous and ready tell them all a few home truths.

Wasn't that why he had lost most of his jobs? For weeks, months on end he would toe the line, dwell on his humiliations, nurse his slights and then, when no one was expecting it, he would explode, almost always for some footling reason – a casual remark, a smile, a trivial contradiction.

'What should I do?' was the question in the inspector's eye.

And the look on André's face replied:

'Wait.'

It did not take long. Like a child's, the crying subsided, almost died away completely, then resumed briefly with increased intensity. Then Olivier snorted, darted a nervous glance all round him and, hiding part of his face, relapsed into what looked like a sulk.

At length he straightened up, bitter and resigned, and declared, though not without pride:

'Ask your questions and I will answer them.'

'What time last night did you go to see Madame Fayet? Wait a second. First tell me what time you left your apartment.'

'At eight, as usual, after putting my son to bed.'

'Did anything unusual happen?'

'No. We ate our suppers together. He helped me to do the washing-up.'

'Did you talk about Christmas?'

'Yes. I more or less told him that there'd be a surprise for him when he woke up in the morning.'

'Was he expecting to get a radio?'

'He's been wanting one for ages. He doesn't play out in the street much, he hasn't got any friends and he spends all his free time at home.'

'Did it never cross your mind that maybe your son knew you'd lost your job with *La Presse*? Didn't he ever need to phone you there?'

'No, never. When I'm at work, he's asleep.'

'Couldn't someone have told him?'

'Where we live, nobody knows.'

'Is he is very observant?'

'He doesn't miss a thing that goes on around us.'

'You tucked him up in bed before you left. Did you pack anything to eat for the night to take with you?'

This thought had only come to the inspector when he saw Godin unwrap a ham sandwich. But Olivier suddenly stared at his empty hands then murmured:

'My box!'

'Is that the box you always use for putting your sandwiches in?'

'Yes. I had it last night, I'm sure. There's only one place where I could have left it.'

'In Madame Fayet's apartment?'

'Yes.'

'One moment . . . Lecœur, put me through to Javel police station . . . Hello? . . . Who's that? . . . Is Janvier there? . . . Get him to come to the phone . . . Is that you, Janvier? . . . Have you searched the old woman's apartment? Have you found a tin box with sandwiches in it? . . . Nothing like that? . . . Are you sure? . . . I'd rather you did, yes . . . Call me back as soon as you've checked . . . It's important . . .'

Then he turned back to Olivier:

'Was your son asleep when you left?'

'He was just about dropping off. We gave each other a kiss. At first, I just walked around the streets nearby for a bit. I went as far as the Seine and sat on the parapet and waited.'

'Waited for what?'

'For François to be fast asleep. From our apartment, you can see Madame Fayet's windows.'

'You'd made up your mind to go and see her?'

'It was the only way. I didn't have enough money to get the Métro.'

'What about your brother?'

The two Lecœurs looked at each other.

'I've I asked him for so much money lately that he can't have much left to spare.'

'Did you ring the front-door bell of her building? What time was it then?'

'Just after nine. The concierge saw me walk past. I never hid, except from my son.'

'Was your mother-in-law still up?'

'Yes. She opened the door and said: "It's you, you swine!"'

'Even so, you knew that she'd let you have the money?'

'I was pretty sure.'

'Why?'

'All I had to do was offer her a fat profit. She could never resist that. I signed a paper stating that I owed her twice as much as she advanced me.'

'Repayable when?'

'In two weeks.'

'And how would you have paid the debt when the two weeks were up?'

'I don't know. I'd have managed somehow. I just wanted my boy to have a happy Christmas.'

André Lecœur felt like interrupting his brother and surprising the inspector by saying: 'He's always been like that!'

'Was it easy to get what you wanted?'

'No. We argued for a long time.'

'For roughly how long?'

'Half an hour. She reminded me that I was a good for nothing so-and-so, that I had brought her daughter nothing but misery, and that it was my fault that she was dead. I didn't answer. I just wanted the money.'

'You didn't threaten her?'

He reddened, lowered his head and stammered:

'I told her that if I didn't get the money, I'd kill myself.'

'Would you have done it?'

'I don't think so. I don't know. I was exhausted and depressed.'

'And when you got the cash?'

'I walked to Beaugrenelle underground station and took the Métro. I got out at Palais Royal and went into Magasins du Louvre. There were a lot of people in the store. There were queues in every department.'

'What time was it then?'

'Around eleven. I was in no hurry. I knew the store stayed open all night. It was warm in there. They had a model electric train that was set up and running.'

His brother gave the inspector a faint smile.

'Didn't you notice that you'd mislaid the box which had your sandwiches in it?'

'I was only thinking about making everything nice for Bott at Christmas.'

'So basically, you were very excited because you had money in your pocket?'

The inspector was not finding it that hard to understand. He didn't need to have known Olivier when he was a boy. Just as he could be depressed and odd and slink along with his shoulders hunched when his pockets were empty, so he could be confident to the point of recklessness the minute he got his hands on a few banknotes.

'You told me you signed an IOU for your mother-in-law. What did she do with it?'

'She put it in an old wallet which she always carried about with her in a bag hanging from a belt which she wore under her skirt.'

'You knew about this wallet?'

'Yes, everyone did.'

The inspector turned to André Lecœur.

'It hasn't been found.'

Then, to Olivier:

'You bought the radio, then the chicken and a cake. Where?'

'On Rue Montmartre, in a shop I know, next door to a place where they sell shoes.'

'What did you do for the rest of the night? What time was it when you left the shop in Rue Montmartre?'

'Almost midnight. Crowds of people were coming out of the theatres and cinemas and heading for the restaurants. There were groups full of high spirits and a lot of couples.'

At that time, his brother was already on duty at his switchboard.

'I found myself on the Grands Boulevards, about level with the Crédit Lyonnais, holding my parcels in both hands, when the bells started ringing. People in the street started kissing each other.'

Why was it that Saillard then felt it was necessary to ask an outrageous, cruel question?

'And did anyone kiss you?'

'No.'

'Did you know where you were going?'

'Yes. There's a cinema showing films non-stop that stays open all night on the corner of Boulevard des Italiens.'

'You'd been there before?'

Visibly embarrassed, he replied, avoiding his brother's eye:

'Two or three times. It doesn't cost more than a cup of coffee in a bar and you can stay there as long as you like. It's warm. Some people go there to sleep.'

'When exactly did you decide to spend the rest of the night in the cinema?'

'As soon as I got the money.'

The other Lecœur, the calm, meticulous man who worked the switchboard, wanted to explain, to tell the inspector:

'Look, these poor down-and-outs aren't as badly off as you might think. If they were, they'd never survive. They have their own world too and in its folds they can find certain small joys . . .'

That was his brother all over! Because he had borrowed a small amount of cash – and how, O Lord! would he ever pay it back? – he had forgotten his troubles and thought only how happy his son would be when he woke up the next morning, yet nevertheless had allowed himself one small treat!

He had gone to the cinema alone, while families gathered around groaning tables, crowds danced in nightclubs and good folk exalted their souls in dimly lit churches where the flames of candles flickered.

And thus it was that he had kept Christmas in his own way, a Christmas made to his measure.

'What time did you leave the cinema?'

'Just before six, when I could use the Métro.'

'What film did you see?'

'*Loving Hearts*. There was also a documentary about the life of Eskimos.'

'Did you see the programme just once?'

'Twice, except for the newsreel, which they were showing again as I left.'

André Lecœur knew that all this would be checked, if only as a matter of routine. But there'd be no need for that. His brother was rummaging through his pockets from which he produced a small piece of torn card, his cinema ticket, together with a second, pink rectangle.

'Ah! There's my Métro ticket too!'

It bore the time, the date and the stamp of the Opéra underground station, where it had been issued.

Olivier had not been lying. He could not have been in old Madame Fayet's bedroom between 5 and 6.30 that morning.

There was now a small gleam of defiance in his eye along with a hint of disdain. He seemed to be telling them, his brother included:

'Because I've never amounted to much, you suspected me. That's standard. I don't hold it against you.'

And then, strangely, they were suddenly aware that it felt colder in the big control room, where one of the telephone operators was talking to a suburban police station about a stolen car.

The reason was probably, now that the problem of Lecœur had been settled, that all thoughts were once more focused on the boy. This refocusing was so undeniable that all eyes turned instinctively to the map of Paris, on which none of the bulbs had lit up for some time.

It was the slow time of day. On another day they might have had the occasional traffic accident, especially involving old ladies knocked over at busy intersections in Montmartre and the more overcrowded parts of the city.

Today, the roads were almost deserted, as they are during the month of August, when most Parisians are away in the country or at the seaside.

It was now 11.30. It was more than three hours since there had been any news of the boy, since the last indication he had given of his movements.

'Hello? Yes . . . I'm listening, Janvier . . . So you're saying there's no tin box in the apartment? . . . Right . . . Was it you who searched the old lady's clothes? . . . Gonesse had already done it before you got there? . . . Are you sure she didn't have an old wallet on a belt under her skirt? Has anyone mentioned it to you? . . . The concierge saw someone going up the stairs last night at about nine thirty? . . . I know who that was . . . Anything else? There were comings and goings in the building all night . . . Obviously . . . Could you go round to the house? . . . The one at the rear, yes . . . I'd like to know if there was any noise there during the night, especially on the third floor . . . Yes, give me a ring . . .'

He turned to Olivier Lecœur, who was once more

sitting motionless on his chair, as self-effacing as a patient in a doctor's waiting room.

'Do you understand the point of my question? . . . Is your son in the habit of waking up during the night?'

'He walks in his sleep sometimes.'

'You mean he gets out of bed and walks around?'

'No. He sits up in bed and screams. It's always the same thing. He thinks the building is on fire. His eyes are wide open, but he doesn't see anything. Then bit by bit his eyes return to normal, and he lies down again with a deep sigh. The next day he doesn't remember a thing.'

'Is he always asleep when you get back in the morning?'

'Not always. But even if he isn't actually sleeping, he pretends to be so that I can wake him up by giving him a kiss and tweaking his nose. It's just a way of showing affection, you see.'

'It's quite likely that the neighbours were making more noise than usual last night. Who lives on the same landing as you?'

'A Czech who works at the car factory.'

'Is he married?'

'I don't know. There are so many people in the building, and tenants move in and out so often that you never really get to know them. On Saturdays, the Czech usually has a half a dozen friends round to drink and sing songs from back home.'

'Janvier is going to phone us back if they had one of their sessions last night. If they did, it might have woken your son. Anyway the prospect of getting the surprise you promised him would have made him excited. If he did get up, he may have gone automatically to the window and seen you in Madame Fayet's apartment. He really had no idea that she was your mother-in-law?'

'No. He didn't like her. He called her Buggy. He often passed her in the street and reckoned she smelled like a squashed bed bug.'

The boy must have been all too familiar with bed bugs, because there was no lack of them in the great barn of a place that they lived in.

'Would he have been surprised to see you in her apartment?'

'Definitely.'

'Did he know she was a money-lender, a loan-shark?'

'Everybody knew.'

The inspector turned to the other Lecœur.

'Do you think anyone will be working at *La Presse* today?'

The answer came from the ex-linotype setter.

'There's always someone there.'

'Well, ring the number. Try and find out if anyone has been asking about Olivier Lecœur.'

Again, Olivier looked away. Before his brother could even open the phone book, he gave him the number of the printing department.

While the phone conversation was going on, all they could do was look at each other and then at the small bulbs which stubbornly refused to light up.

'It's very important, mademoiselle. It could be a matter of life and death . . . I do assure you! . . . Please would you be good enough to ask everyone who's there at the moment . . . What's that? . . . I can't help it! It's Christmas for me too but I'm at work phoning you . . .'

'Stupid cow!' André muttered between his teeth.

And again they waited while the rattle of linotype machines sounded tinnily in the receiver.

'Hello! . . . What? . . . Three weeks ago? . . . A boy, yes . . .'

The father had turned pale and was staring at his hands.

'He didn't phone? He came in person? At about what time of day? . . . A Thursday? What happened? . . . He asked if Olivier Lecœur worked on the presses . . . How come? . . . What was he told? . . .'

Olivier looked up and saw his brother's face flush red as he slammed the receiver down angrily.

'Your son went there one Thursday afternoon . . . He must have suspected something . . . He was told that you hadn't worked at *La Presse* for weeks.'

What purpose would have been served by repeating the exact words he had just heard? What the boy had been told was:

'It's ages since the idiot was given the sack!'

Maybe it was not cruelly meant. Probably no one had thought that the boy might be his son.

'Are you beginning to understand, Olivier?'

Every evening, he had left, taking his sandwiches with him, saying he was going off to the printing works in Rue du Croissant, and each time the boy had known he was lying.

Should they not conclude that he also knew the truth about wonderful Uncle Gideon?

He had gone along with the lies.

'And I promised I'd get him his radio . . .'

They hardly dared speak, because any words they could say might conjure up frightening images.

Even those who had never set foot in Rue Vasco-de-Gama could now picture the shabby apartment and the ten-year-old boy who spent long hours there by himself and imagine the strange relationship of father and son, who both lived lies because they were afraid of hurting each other.

They should have been able to see things through a child's eyes: his father leaving after bending over his bed to kiss him on the forehead, and the fact that it was Christmas everywhere, with the neighbours drinking and singing their songs at the tops of their voices.

'Tomorrow you'll get a big surprise!'

It could only have been the radio he'd dreamed of, and Bott knew exactly how much it cost. Did he also know that on that Christmas Eve his father's wallet was empty?

His father went out as if he were going to work, though he no longer had a job. Had the boy tried to go to sleep? Outside his bedroom, on the opposite side of the courtyard rose a towering wall punctuated by the brightly lit rectangles of windows and the variegated life that went on behind them.

Couldn't he have leaned on his elbows, in his night clothes, and looked out?

His father, who had no money, was going to buy him a radio.

The inspector gave a sigh as he knocked out his pipe on the heel of his shoe, dumping its contents straight on to the floor.

'It's more than probable that he saw you in the old girl's apartment.'

'Yes.'

'There's one detail I shall want to check later. You live on the third floor, and her apartment was on the mezzanine. It's quite likely that only part of her bedroom is visible from your windows.'

'That's correct.'

'Could your son have seen you leave her apartment?'

'No. Her front door is at the far side of the room.'

'Did you stand near the window?'

'I sat on the window-sill.'

'One thing that might be important: was the window partly open?'

'It was. I remember, it was like having a freezing-cold stripe all down my back. My mother-in-law has always slept with a window open, winter and summer. She was a country woman. She lived with us for a while immediately after we got married.'

The inspector turned to the man at the switchboard.

'Did you think of that, Lecœur?'

'You mean the frost on the window? I've been thinking about it since this morning. If the window was partly open, the difference between the temperature outside and the temperature in the room would not have been great enough for frost to form.'

A report coming in. The jack went straight into one of the sockets.

'Yes . . . What's that? . . . A boy?'

The men in the room watched him intently.

'Yes . . . Yes . . . What? . . . Of course, get all your mounted men out on their bikes searching the area . . . I'm covering the station . . . How long ago was that? . . . Half an hour? . . . Couldn't he have let us know sooner? . . .'

Without taking time to explain to his colleagues, Lecœur thrust a jack into another socket.

'Gare du Nord? . . . Who's that? . . . Lambert? . . . Listen, this is very urgent . . . I want you to have the station thoroughly searched . . . I want a watch kept on all enclosed places and all tracks. Ask the station staff if they have seen a boy about ten years old hanging around the ticket barriers or anywhere else . . . Sorry? . . . If there's a grown-up with him? . . . Whatever you have to . . . It's quite possible . . . Get on to it! . . . Keep me posted . . . Of course, grab hold of him . . .'

'A grown-up with him?' repeated Olivier with alarm.

'Why not? We can't rule anything out. It may not be him, but if it is, the trail is half an hour cold . . . It was a grocer in Rue de Maubeuge, just opposite Gare du Nord. He's got an outside sales counter . . . He saw a boy snatch a couple of oranges from his display and run away . . . He didn't give chase . . . Only some time later, when he saw a uniformed officer across the road, did he report it, said it was his civic duty . . .'

'Did your son have any money on him?' asked the inspector. 'No? Does he have a money-box?'

'He's got one. But I took everything in it, it wasn't much, two days ago. I told him I didn't want to change a large note.'

How important were such small details becoming now!

'Don't you think I'd be more useful if I went and had a look round Gare du Nord myself?'

'I don't believe that would serve any useful purpose whatsoever. Besides we might need you here.'

They were in a sense prisoners in this room, chained to the large wall map with its winking lights and the switchboard which connected them to all parts of Paris. Whatever happened, they would be the first to know. The inspector was so aware of this that he decided not to go back to his own office and finally discarded his thick overcoat, as if he were a member of the control-room staff.

'So he couldn't take the Métro or get on a bus. Nor could he go into a café or a public phone box to ring us. He hasn't eaten anything since six this morning.'

'But what's he up to?' cried his father, growing excited again. 'And why did he tell me to go to Gare d'Austerlitz?'

'Probably to help you escape,' said Saillard softly.

'Me, escape?'

'Now listen to me . . .'

The inspector was forgetting that Olivier was the brother of Inspector Lecœur and was talking to him as if he were just another 'customer'.

'He knows you're out of a job, you're broke and yet you promise him a right royal Christmas . . .'

'My mother also used to go without for months so we wouldn't be disappointed on Christmas Day . . .'

'I'm not blaming you, only stating the obvious. He leans on the window-sill and sees you with this old blood-sucking money-lender. What do you think he makes of it?'

'I see your point.'

'He tells himself that you've gone there to borrow money. Fine. Maybe he's touched. Perhaps he feels sad, I have no idea. He gets into bed again and goes back to sleep.'

'You really think so?'

'I'm pretty certain. If at nine thirty last night he had found out what he discovered at six this morning, he wouldn't have stayed quietly in his room.'

'I understand.'

'So he goes back to sleep. Perhaps he thinks more about his radio than about what you did to get the money for it. You yourself went to the cinema, didn't you? He doesn't sleep very well the night before Christmas, just like other children. He wakes up earlier than usual, when it's still dark, and the first thing he notices is that ice has formed on the inside of the windows. Don't forget that it's the first frost we've had this winter. He wanted to see it close up, to touch it . . .'

The other Lecœur, the one with the phone jacks, the one who made little crosses in a notebook, gave a faint smile as he realized that the burly inspector was not as far removed from his childhood as might have been thought.

'He scraped the pane with his fingernails.'

'Just the way I saw Bigue do it this morning, here, in this room,' broke in André Lecœur.

'If it becomes necessary, we'll know for sure one way

or another from the Criminal Records team, because once frost melts we should get fingerprints. What is it that grabs the boy's attention? Though it's completely dark everywhere in the neighbourhood, one window is lit up, just one, and it's the window of the room where he last saw his father. I'll have all these details checked. But I'd swear he saw the corpse, either all or part of it. Even if he saw just the feet on the floor. And that, plus the fact that the room was brightly lit, would have been enough . . .'

'For him to believe? . . .' began Olivier, his eyes starting out of his head.

'To believe you'd killed her, yes, just as I almost believed it too. Think, Lecœur. A man who has been committing murders in the outer suburbs of Paris, for several weeks now, lives at night, like you. He's probably someone who has had a terrible shock, just like you, because people do not start killing from one day to the next for no reason. Did your son know what you've been doing every night since you lost your job?'

He went on:

'You told us earlier that you were sitting on the window-sill. Where did you leave the box with your sandwiches in?'

'On the window-sill beside me, I'm pretty sure . . .'

'So he saw it . . . And he didn't know at what time you left your mother-in-law's apartment . . . He didn't know if she was still alive after you'd gone . . . He must have believed that the electric light had been on all night . . .

'If you'd been him, what's the first thing you'd have noticed?'

'My sandwich box . . .'

'Precisely. The box the police would use to identify you. Is your name on it?'

'I scratched it on with a penknife.'

'You see? Your son assumed that you would come home at the usual time, that is, between seven and eight o'clock in the morning. He didn't know if his plan would work. But in any case he didn't want to go back home. What he was trying to do was to keep you away from danger.'

'Was that why he left me a note?'

'He remembered Uncle Gideon. He wrote telling you that he was due to arrive at Gare d'Austerlitz. He knew you'd go there even though there was no such person. The note wouldn't implicate you in any way . . .'

'He's only ten and a half!' protested his father.

'There's no reason to think a kid of ten and a half knows any less about these things than you do! Doesn't he read detective stories?'

'Yes . . .'

'Perhaps the reason he wants a radio so much is less for the music or the plays they broadcast than for the detective serials . . .'

'You're right.'

'His first and most urgent task was to retrieve the incriminating box. He was familiar with the courtyard. He often played there.'

'He used to spend days and days down in that yard, with the concierge's little girl.'

'Therefore he must have known he could use the drain-pipe. Maybe he'd climbed up it before.'

'What then?' asked Olivier, now impressively calm. 'So he retrieved my box. He had no problem getting out of my mother-in-law's apartment, because the front door opens from inside, so there was no need to call the concierge. You said it would then be just after six this morning.'

'I see where this is leading,' growled the inspector. 'Even if he didn't hurry, it wouldn't have taken him two hours to get to Gare d'Austerlitz, where he had arranged to meet you. So that's not where he went.'

Ignoring their theorizing, André Lecœur pushed his jack home and spoke softly:

'It's me. Still nothing?'

And the voice from Gare du Nord replied:

'We've already questioned a couple of dozen adults who were with children, but none of them answered the description you circulated.'

Obviously, any kid could steal oranges from a grocer's stall. But not just any kid would have smashed the glass of seven emergency phones one after the other. Lecœur kept going back to his little crosses. He had never believed he was much smarter than his brother, but he had patience and tenacity on his side.

'I'm convinced,' he said, 'that we'll find the sandwich box in the Seine, under Pont Mirabeau.'

Footsteps on the stairs outside. On ordinary days, no one would pay them any attention. But on Christmas Day, people listen out for such things almost unconsciously.

It was a police messenger who had come by bicycle, bringing the blood-stained handkerchief which had been found next to the seventh emergency phone. They held it out for the boy's father to see.

'Yes, it's Bott's.'

'That means that he was being followed,' said the inspector. 'If he hadn't been, if he'd had time, he wouldn't have just broken the glass, he'd have used the phones to say something.'

'I'm not with you,' said Olivier who was the only one there who had not understood. 'Followed by whom? And why would he call the police?'

No one rushed to tell him, to put him wise. It was his brother who stepped up to the plate.

'Because when he climbed into Madame Fayet's apartment, he thought you were the murderer. But by the time he left he no longer thought that. *He knew . . .*'

'Knew what?'

'He knew *who*! Has the penny dropped yet? He found out something, we don't know what, but what it was is precisely what we've been trying to discover all this time. But someone is not giving him a chance to tell us.'

'You mean? . . .'

'I mean either your son is following the murderer or the murderer is following him. One of them is following the other. I don't know which way round, but whoever the man is, he has no intention of giving up. Tell me, inspector, has a reward been offered?'

'A large reward was offered after the third murder. It was doubled last week. It was in all the papers.'

'So,' said André Lecœur, 'Bott isn't necessarily the one being followed. He could be the one who's doing the following. But in that case . . .'

It was now noon, and four hours since the boy had given any sign of life – unless, that is, he was the little thief who had stolen the two oranges in Rue de Maubeuge.

4.

Could it be, all things considered, that his day had come? André Lecœur had read somewhere that at least once in the life of all human beings, however dull or unfortunate they might be, there comes a moment of glory when they are given the opportunity to maximize their potential.

He had never had a very high opinion of himself or his potential. If anyone asked him why he had chosen a monotonous, sedentary job instead, for example, of applying to join the Murder Squad, he always replied:

'I'm far too lazy!'

Sometimes he would add:

'And maybe I'm scared of getting hurt.'

That was not true. But he was aware that his mind worked slowly.

Everything he had learned in school had cost him considerable effort. The police exams, which for others were child's play, had given him no end of trouble.

Was it because he knew himself so well that he had never married? Possibly. He felt that whatever the woman he asked to be his wife was like, he would feel inferior and end up under her thumb.

He was not thinking of such things now. He had no sense that perhaps his big moment was imminent – if indeed he was to have one.

A new team, this one fresh and sprucely turned-out, a team which had had time to celebrate Christmas with their families, had just replaced the morning shift, and there was a smell of cake and liqueurs on their breath.

Bedeau, an old hand, was about to take his place at the switchboard, but Lecœur was still there and said simply:

'I'll stay on for a while.'

Inspector Saillard had gone out to grab a quick lunch in the Brasserie Dauphine around the corner, leaving word that he should be called if anything new turned up. Janvier had gone back to Quai des Orfèvres, where he was writing his report.

Lecœur did not want to go home to bed. He did not feel at all tired. Once he had remained at his post for thirty-six hours on the trot when there had been riots on Place de la Concorde. And on another occasion, during the general strikes, the staff manning the central switchboard had not left the building for four days and four nights.

His brother was much more impatient:

'I want to go out and look for Bott!' he had exclaimed.

'Where?'

'I don't know. Around Gare du Nord.'

'What if it wasn't him who stole the oranges? What if he's in another part of town altogether? What if we hear from him in a couple of minutes or a couple of hours?'

'I just want to do something.'

They had sat him down on a chair in a corner of the room because he refused to see sense. His eyes were red-rimmed with fatigue and worry and he started pulling on his fingers the way he used to when he was a boy and had been told to stand in the corner.

André Lecœur had forced himself to try to get some rest. Just off the large control room there was a cubicle of sorts with a wash-basin, two camp beds and a clothes stand where men on the night shift sometimes went for a nap when there was a lull.

He had closed his eyes. Then his hand reached into his pocket for the notebook he always kept by him and, lying on his back, he began turning its pages.

It contained only crosses, columns of minute crosses which over many years he had gone on marking without anybody telling him to, without having any idea what use they might be one day. Some people keep a diary. For others, it's a record of every last penny they spend or their losses at bridge.

Those crosses in narrow columns represented years of the life of Paris by night.

'Fancy some coffee, Lecœur?'

'Please.'

But feeling too isolated in the cubicle, from which he could not see the wall map and its little lights, he dragged the camp bed into the control room, drank his coffee and then passed the time scrutinizing the crosses in his log-book and closing his eyes. From time to time, through his half-closed lids, he would peer out at his brother, who sat slumped on a chair, shoulders down, head bent, offering only one outward sign of his inner turmoil: the convulsive clenching and unclenching of his long pale fingers.

The number of officers not just in central Paris but in

the suburbs who had been given the boy's description now ran into the hundreds. There was a glimmer of hope from time to time. A police station would call in, but only to report a sighting of a little girl or a boy who was too young or too old.

Lecœur was closing his eyes again but suddenly opened them as though he had just been dropping off. He glanced at the time and looked around him for the inspector.

'Isn't Saillard back yet?'

'He has probably called in at Quai des Orfèvres.'

Olivier looked up at him, surprised to see him striding around the huge room. Lecœur hardly noticed that outside the sun had finally broken through the white dome of cloud and that on this Christmas afternoon Paris was brightly lit and almost springlike.

What he was listening out for was the sound of footsteps on the stairs.

'Why don't you go out and buy some sandwiches,' he said to his brother.

'What sort?'

'Ham. Any sort. Whatever you can find.'

Olivier left the control room after one last look at the map on the wall, glad despite his anxiety to be going out for a moment to get a breath of fresh air.

The men who had replaced the morning team knew hardly anything, except that something was going on about the killer and that somewhere in Paris a small boy was in danger. For those who had not spent the night here, the situation did not have the same feel about it and had been filtered, reduced to a small number of precise, cold facts. The experienced Bedeau, now in Lecœur's seat, was doing a crossword with his headphones clamped to his head and scarcely interrupted his train of thought to breathe the ritual:

'Hello? Austerlitz? Has your van been called out?'

A corpse had just been fished out of the Seine – this too was part of the Christmas tradition.

'Could I have a quick word with you, sir?'

The camp bed had been returned to its rightful place in the cubicle, and it was there that Lecœur led the chief of the Murder Squad. The inspector was smoking his pipe and as he took off his overcoat he gave his junior a look of surprise.

'I'm sorry to poke my nose into what is none of my business. It's about the killer . . .'

He had his little notebook in his hand, though it looked as if he knew its contents by heart and only consulted it for form's sake.

'I apologize if what I'm going to say about certain thoughts that I've been having comes out as a jumble, but I've been going over and over it so many times since this morning that . . .'

Earlier, when he'd been lying down, it had all seemed so clear in his mind that he had been dazzled by it. Now, he struggled to find his words and the ideas, which were becoming more elusive.

'Right, then! The first thing I would point out is that all eight murders were committed after two in the morning and the majority after three . . .'

He could tell by the look on the inspector's face that for

other people this observation was not exactly earth-shattering.

'I was curious and checked up on the times when most crimes of this sort were committed over the last three years. It was almost invariably between ten o'clock at night and two in the morning.'

He must have got off on the wrong foot for he elicited no reaction whatsoever. Why not come out frankly about how he had got the idea? This was no time to let himself be stopped by being coy.

'A little while back, I took a good look at my brother and thought that the man you're looking for is probably someone very like him. For a moment I even wondered if it wasn't actually him. Wait a second . . .'

He felt he was on the right track now. He had seen in the inspector's eyes something more than just polite, perfunctory attention.

'If I'd had enough time, I would have put my ideas in order. But just wait and see . . . A man who kills eight times, virtually one after the other, is a lunatic, isn't he? . . . He is someone who, for some reason or other, blows a fuse overnight . . .

'My brother lost his job and to avoid admitting it to his son, to prevent himself looking small in his eyes, he went on for weeks leaving home at the usual time and behaving exactly as if he was in work . . .'

When put into words and sentences like this, the idea lost much of its force. He could see that while Saillard was obviously making an effort, he did not have an inkling about where all this was leading.

'A man who suddenly has taken from him everything he had, everything that was his life . . .'

'And goes mad?'

'I don't know if he's mad, sir. But maybe "mad" is the word for it. Someone who believes he has every reason for hating the whole world, for wanting to get even with the rest of humanity . . .

'As you of course know, sir, the other kind, the real murderers, always kill in the same way.

'But the man you're looking for has used a knife, a hammer and a wrench. He strangled one of the women.

'And not once has he let himself be seen. Nowhere has he left any trace. Wherever he lives, he must have covered many kilometres in Paris at times when there were no buses or Métro trains running. And although the police have been on the look-out for him since the first murders, scrutinizing passers-by and arresting suspicious characters, he has not put his head above the parapet one single time.'

He was so confident he was now on the right track, but at the same time so afraid that the inspector would get tired of listening, that he almost felt like making a direct appeal to him:

'Please hear me out!'

The cubicle was so small that he could take only three steps in each direction while the inspector sat on the edge of the camp bed.

'None of this is speculation, believe me. I'm incapable of working out clever theories. Instead, I rely on my little crosses, they are facts which I have recorded . . .

'This morning, for example, he crossed half of Paris without walking past one police station, without going via a single roundabout or intersection where there was a policeman on duty.'

'Are you sure he knows the fifteenth arrondissement like the back of his hand?'

'Not only the fifteenth but at least two others, the twentieth and the twelfth, if you go by the earlier murders. He doesn't choose his victims at random. In every case, he has known that they were solitary women living in circumstances which enabled him to attack them without risk to himself.'

His heart sank when he heard his brother's dreary voice:

'I've got the sandwiches, André!'

'Good! Thanks. Have one yourself. Go and sit down . . .'

He did not dare close the door, he was too diffident for that. He ranked too low to shut himself away with an inspector.

'If he uses a different weapon each time, it's because he realizes it will muddy his tracks, which means that he *knows* that murderers in general stick to one method.'

'Look, Lecœur . . .'

The inspector had just got to his feet and was looking at him glassy-eyed, as if he was now following a line of thought of his own.

'What exactly,' he said, 'are you telling me?'

'I'm not sure. But it did cross my mind that he could be one of us. Someone at any rate who has worked in the force.'

He lowered his voice.

'Somebody who has been through the same experience as my brother, don't you see? A firefighter who's been sacked might just as easily decide to start fires. It's happened twice in the last three years. Someone in the police force . . .'

'But why does he steal?'

'My brother also needed money, to make his son believe he was continuing to work for his living, that he was still regularly employed at *La Presse*. Now if our man worked nights and is letting someone think he still has a job, then by definition he stays out all night, and that explains why he commits his murders after three in the morning. He has to wait until morning before he can go home. The first hours are no problem: there are cafés and bars that stay open. But after that he is all alone on the streets.'

Saillard muttered, almost to himself:

'There won't be anybody in Personnel today . . .'

'Maybe it would be possible to get on to the director at home? Perhaps he can remember.'

Lecœur was not done yet. There were still many things he would like to have said but they escaped him. Perhaps it was all nothing more than a fanciful product of his imagination. It certainly seemed that way to him at times. But at others, he felt he had come up with something that was blindingly obvious.

'Hello? Could I speak to Monsieur Guillaume, please? . . . He's not at home? Do you know where I could contact him? . . . At his daughter's at Auteuil? You wouldn't have the phone number?'

Here were other people who had sat down to a good lunch as a family and were now probably sipping coffee and liqueurs.

'Monsieur Guillaume? It's Saillard, yes. I hope I'm not disturbing you too much . . . You've finished lunch? I'm ringing about the killer. There has been a development . . . Nothing definite as yet. I'd like to test a theory, and it's urgent. Don't be too surprised by my question. Has any member of the police force, of any rank, been dismissed from his post in the last few months? . . . I didn't quite catch . . . Not one in the last year?'

Lecœur felt his chest tighten as if he expected some catastrophe to overwhelm him. He cast a despairing look at the map of Paris. His gamble had backfired. He decided not to play any more such games and so was surprised to hear his chief insisting:

'Perhaps it was more than a year ago, I don't know. It would be a man regularly on the night shift in several arrondissements, including the fifteenth, twentieth and twelfth. A man whose dismissal left him very bitter . . . What? . . .'

The tone of Saillard's voice which had pronounced this last word gave Lecœur fresh hope, while all around them the other men did not understand the significance of Saillard's conversation.

'Sergeant Loubet? . . . Actually, I did hear about him but I wasn't a member of the disciplinary board at the time . . . Three years, yes . . . You wouldn't happen to know where he lived? . . . Somewhere near Les Halles?'

Three years! It didn't fit! Lecœur's spirits sank once

more. It was very unlikely that a man would keep his humiliation and hatred on the boil for three years before he did anything about them.

'You wouldn't happen to know what became of him? . . . Yes, that will be difficult today . . .'

He replaced the receiver and gave Lecœur a searching look. Then he spoke to him as though he were talking to an equal.

'You heard that? It was about a sergeant named Loubet who was given a series of warnings and was moved three or four times from one station to another before being sacked. He took it very badly. He drank. Guillaume thinks he found a job with a private security firm. You could always try to . . .'

Lecœur set about it without conviction, but it meant doing something rather than just sitting and waiting in front of the indispensable wall map. He started with the shadiest firms, on the premise that a man like Loubet would not have been employed by a reputable company. Most of the offices were closed. He rang people at home.

He often heard children's voices.

'Never heard of him. You could try Tisserand's, on Boulevard Saint-Martin. They take on the barrel-scrapings.'

But he also drew a blank at Tisserand's which specialized in having people followed.

Lecœur had been glued to the same phone for three-quarters of an hour when at last he heard someone snap angrily:

'Don't talk to me about that waster! It's more than two months since I gave him his marching orders. He threatened to blackmail me, but he hasn't done a thing about it. If I ever see him again, I'll smash his face in for him.'

'What sort of work did he do for you?'

'He was a night watchman.'

André Lecœur's face was completely transformed again.

'Did he drink much?'

'Let's say that he was drunk after he'd been on duty for less than an hour. I don't know how he worked it, but he somehow managed to get all his drinks without paying for them.'

'Do you have his exact address?'

'27A, Rue du Pas-de-la-Mule.'

'Does he have a phone?'

'Probably. I have absolutely no wish to speak to him. Is that all? Can I get back to my game of bridge now?'

Then as the man was hanging up, he could be heard telling his friends all about it.

The inspector had already reached for the phone book and had located Loubet's name. He dialled the number. There was now between him and André Lecœur a kind of tacit understanding. They were both hoping for the same thing. And now, as they were closing in on their target, they had the same tingling in their fingertips. Meanwhile the other Lecœur – Olivier – sensing that something important was happening, was on his feet watching both of them in turn.

Without being asked, André Lecœur did something which as late as that morning he would never have dreamed of doing: he picked up the other earphone. There was the sound of a phone ringing at the other end of the line in the apartment in Rue du Pas-de-la-Mule. It rang and rang in what seemed like a vacuum. Lecœur's chest was beginning to tighten when someone picked up the receiver.

Thank God!

It was the voice of an elderly woman. It said:

'Is that you at long last? Where are you?'

'Good afternoon, madame. This isn't your husband speaking.'

'Has he had an accident?'

It seemed from the tone of her voice that she found the thought distinctly attractive, and that she had been expecting it for a very long time.

'Am I speaking to Madame Loubet?'

'And who might you be?'

'Is your husband not at home?'

'Tell me first who this is.'

'Inspector Saillard . . .'

'Why do you want to speak to him?'

The inspector covered the mouthpiece briefly with his hand and whispered to Lecœur:

'Ring Janvier and tell him to get round there as soon as he can.'

A police station called in at the same moment, so that now there were three phones operating in the room.

'Hasn't your husband returned this morning?'

'If the police knew what they were doing, you wouldn't have to ask.'

'Does it happen often?'

'Why is that any of your business?'

She probably hated her drunkard of a husband, but as soon as anyone attacked him she stood up for him.

'You do know that he is no longer a part of the police force, don't you?'

'He's not so useless as to do that!'

'When exactly did he stop working for Argus Security?'

'What? . . . Just a moment, please . . . What did you say? . . . Don't think you can worm anything out of me . . .'

'I'm sorry, madame, but it's more than two months since your husband was dismissed by Argus.'

'You're lying!'

'In other words, you're saying that for the last two months your husband has been going off every night to his place of work?'

'Where else would he have gone? The Folies-Bergère?'

'Why hasn't he come home this morning? Hasn't he phoned you?'

She was probably scared of being caught off her guard, because she simply hung up.

When the inspector had also replaced the receiver at his end, he saw André Lecœur standing behind him. As he turned, Lecœur said:

'Janvier is on his way there now . . .'

And with one finger he wiped away a drop of moisture from the corner of his eye.

5.

They now treated each other exactly as equals. He knew it would not last, that tomorrow he would be just a very ordinary telephone operator sitting at his switchboard, an odd character who wrote down little crosses in a little notebook that served no useful purpose.

The other men didn't matter. He wasn't even worrying about his brother, who watched each of them in turn with shy, rabbit's eyes, overheard them speaking without understanding what they said and wondered why, when his son's life was at stake, they talked so much and did nothing.

Twice he tugged at André's sleeve:

'Let me go out and look for him . . .' he begged.

Look where? Look for who? The description of ex-Sergeant Loubet had already been circulated to all police stations, railway terminals and all patrols.

The police were not just looking for a boy now but for a man of fifty-eight, probably drunk, who knew Paris inside out and the capital's police force like the back of his hand and was wearing a black overcoat with a velvet collar and an old grey fedora.

Janvier had come back looking fresher than the others. Actually, all the new men who arrived now remained for some time wreathed in an aura of freshness which they had brought in with them from outside. Then they too gradually slipped into the cloud of all-encompassing greyness which made it seem that life was being lived in slow motion.

'She tried to shut the door in my face but I'd taken the precaution of sticking my foot in it. She doesn't know anything. She says that in the last few months he's been handing over his pay as usual.'

'That's why he had to steal! He didn't need a lot of money, he wouldn't have known what to do with it. What's she like?'

'Short and sallow-skinned, with quick, darting eyes and hair dyed almost blue. She probably has eczema or some sort of skin rash, because she wears mittens.'

'Did you get a photo of him?'

'I almost had to use force to confiscate it from the side-board in the dining room.

A thickset, florid-faced man with deep-set eyes who had probably been cock-of-the-walk in his village when he was young and now looked stupid and arrogant. But the photo was several years old. By this time of life, Loubet would certainly have gone to seed, his body sagging and the self-assurance replaced by a degree of low cunning.

'Did you manage to find out where his usual haunts are?'

'As far as I could make out, she keeps a tight rein on him, except at night when he is out at work – or she assumes he is. I questioned the concierge. He's terrified of his wife. Often, in the morning, the concierge sees him staggering home but he straightens himself up the moment his hand touches the banister of the stairs. He goes shopping with his wife and never goes out during the day unless she's with him. When he sleeps in the daytime and she has errands to run, she locks him in and takes the key with her.'

'What do you reckon, Lecœur?'

'I'm wondering if my nephew and he are together.'

'What are you getting at?'

'They weren't together at the start, around six thirty this morning, because Loubet would have stopped the kid smashing the glass of the emergency phones. There was some distance between them. One of them was following the other.'

'Which was which in your view?'

It was disconcerting to be listened to in this way, as if he had suddenly turned into some kind of oracle. He had never felt as unsure of himself in his life, so terrified was he of being wrong.

'When François climbed up the drainpipe, he believed his father was guilty. That's why he used the note and the tale of Uncle Gideon to send him scuttling off to Gare d'Austerlitz where he clearly planned to meet up with him after getting rid of the sandwich box.'

'That seems plausible to me . . .'

'Bott would never have believed I . . .' Olivier tried to object.

'Don't interrupt! . . . At that point, the murder had only just been committed. If the boy hadn't seen the corpse, he wouldn't have shinned up the drainpipe.'

'He did see it,' Janvier broke in. 'From his window, he could see the body from the feet to halfway up the thighs.'

'What we don't know is whether or not the man was still in the room.'

'But we do!' said the inspector. 'If he had been, he would have stayed hidden while the boy climbed in through the window and then eliminated a dangerous witness the same way he had dispatched the old woman.'

But they would have to understand everything down to the last detail, reconstitute exactly what had happened, if they were to find young François Lecœur, who had two radio sets, not one, waiting for him as his Christmas present.

'Listen, Olivier, when you got back home this morning, was the light on?'

'Yes.'

'Also in the boy's bedroom?'

'Yes. It gave me a shock. I thought he was ill.'

'So the killer could have seen the light in Bott's window. He was afraid there was a witness. He wouldn't have thought for a moment that anyone could get into the room by climbing up the drainpipe. He got out of the building fast . . .'

'And waited outside to see what would happen.'

It was all they could do: conjecture, resort to human logic in so far as was possible. The rest had to be left to the patrols, to hundreds of policemen scattered throughout Paris – in other words to chance.

'Rather than leave by the way he had got in, the boy walked out of the old woman's apartment through the front door . . .'

'One moment, inspector. At that point, he probably knew his father wasn't the murderer.'

'Why?'

'Earlier, I heard someone say, I think it was Janvier, that old Madame Fayet had lost a lot of blood. If the crime had just been committed, the blood would not be dry yet, and the body would still be warm. Now Bott had seen his father in her bedroom the previous evening at around nine o'clock . . .'

With every new inference came fresh hope. They felt they were making progress. What remained to be done began to look easier. There were times when the two men opened their mouths simultaneously to speak, as though both had been struck by the same thought.

'It was when the boy left the building that he saw the man, who was either Loubet or possibly somebody else, though it was probably Loubet. But whoever it was wouldn't have been sure whether his face had been seen or not. The boy was frightened and made himself scarce . . .'

This time, it was Olivier who interrupted. He disagreed and went on in an even voice:

'Not if Bott knew there was a large reward. Not if he knew I'd lost my job. Not if he'd seen me trying to borrow money from my mother-in-law . . .'

The inspector and André exchanged glances and because they sensed that the boy's father was right, they both felt afraid at the same moment.

It was the stuff of nightmares: an empty street in one of the most run-down parts of Paris, in the dead of night with still two hours to go before it would start to get light . . .

On one hand a maniac who had just killed for the eighth time in a matter of weeks, a man motivated by hatred, contempt, by compulsion too, and maybe also by a need to prove God knows what to himself, a man who used what remained of his pride to defy the universe by pitting himself against the police.

Was he drunk, as he normally was? Since it was Christmas Eve, when the bars stay open all night, it was more than likely that he'd had even more to drink than usual and was seeing everything through alcohol-fuddled eyes. And what he saw in that street, in that wilderness of stone, between those unseeing walls was a child, a boy, who could get him arrested and put an end to his murderous rampages.

'I'd like to know if he had a revolver,' the inspector said tentatively.

He did not have to wait long for an answer. It came immediately from Janvier.

'I asked his wife about that. He always carried an automatic, but it wasn't loaded.'

'Why was that?'

'His wife was afraid of him. When he'd had too much to drink, instead of doing what she told him to, he sometimes turned on her. She had locked the cartridges away, saying that if the need arose, the gun would be enough by itself to scare anyone off, and he wouldn't have to fire it.'

Had the two of them, the crazed old man and the young kid, then begun playing a game of cat and mouse through the streets of Paris? The former police sergeant could not hope to outrun a boy of ten. But neither could the boy hope to overpower a man of his size.

But for François, that man represented a fortune, he meant an end to all their money troubles. His father would no longer have to roam the streets at night pretending that he still had a job in Rue du Croissant, or lug vegetables around Les Halles, or go cap in hand to Madame Fayet to beg for a loan he couldn't ever repay.

The waiting men had no need to speak much now. They stared at the wall map and the names of the streets. No doubt the boy was keeping a safe distance from the murderer, and it was equally likely that the man had brandished his gun to frighten him.

In every nook and cranny of every house and tenement in the city, thousands of people slept and could not be of any help to either of them.

Loubet could not stay out on the street indefinitely, keeping an eye on the boy, who carefully kept his distance, so he had started walking, avoiding dangerous streets, the blue lamp outside each police station and all intersections where police were on duty.

In two hours, three at most, there would be people about in the streets and no doubt the kid would rush up to the first person he met and ask for help.

'So it was Loubet who started walking first?' the inspector said slowly.

'And as my nephew followed, he started smashing the glass fronts of emergency police phones because I had explained to him how they work,' added André Lecœur.

The little crosses now began to acquire a life of their own. What in the beginning had been a mystery had now become very simple, but potentially tragic.

Though perhaps the most tragic thing of all was the matter of that large sum of money, the reward, for which a boy of ten had subjected himself to terror and put his life at risk.

Olivier began to cry, not sobbing, not weeping noisily but gently, making no effort to hide his tears. There were no more nervous antics now, no more outbursts. He was in unfamiliar surroundings, full of impersonal machines and men who talked about him as if he was someone else, as if he wasn't there, and his brother was one of those men, a brother he hardly recognized but automatically looked up to.

The snatches of conversation became briefer, because Lecœur and the inspector understood each other perfectly.

'Loubet couldn't go home . . .'

'Or walk into a bar, not with the kid hot on his tail . . .'

And then, André Lecœur gave a sudden, involuntary smile.

'It never occurred to our man that the kid had no money in his pocket so that he could have shaken him off just by taking the Métro!'

But wait! That did not stand up. Bott had seen him and could give an accurate description of him.

Trocadéro. The area around the Arc de Triomphe. Time had passed. It was almost light. People had started coming out of their houses. Footsteps sounded on pavements.

It was no longer possible, without a blade, to kill a child in the street without attracting attention.

'One way or another, they are now together,' said the inspector decisively with a shake of his head, as though he was just waking from a nightmare.

At that moment a light flashed on. As if he knew that the call would be about their case, Lecœur himself answered, not his colleague.

'Yes . . . I thought as much . . . Thanks.'

He explained:

'It was about those two oranges. They've just found a young North African boy sleeping in the third-class waiting room at Gare du Nord. He still had one of the oranges in his pocket. He ran away this morning from home in the eighteenth arrondissement, because he had been knocked about.'

'Do you think Bott is dead?'

Olivier Lecœur pulled on his fingers hard enough to break them.

'If he was dead, Loubet would have gone home, because he wouldn't have had anything more to fear.'

And so the struggle went on in a – finally – sunlit Paris, where families were strolling out in their Sunday best with their children.

'Bott probably used the crowd to close the gap between them, because he was afraid of losing the trail.'

Loubet must have managed to speak to him and threaten him with his gun: 'If you yell, I shoot!'

In this way they were both following their own agendas: one, to get rid of the kid by dragging him into a deserted alley where he could do away with him; the other, to raise the alarm before the man had time to fire his gun.

Each was wary of the other, and both were gambling with their lives.

'Obviously Loubet wouldn't have headed towards the centre of Paris, where there are too many policemen about. All the more so because most of them know him by sight.'

From the Arc de Triomphe they must have gone back up to Montmartre, not the Montmartre of the nightclubs but to the unglamorous back streets which, on a day like this, were at their most provincial.

It was now two thirty. Had they eaten anything? Had Loubet, despite the threat hanging over him, managed to go all this time without a drink?

'Can I say something, inspector . . .?'

For all his best efforts, André Lecœur could not speak with any confidence. He could not shake off the impression that he was trespassing on territory where he had no right to be.

'There are hundreds of small bars in Paris, I know. But if we start with the most likely locations, and if we put enough men on the job . . .'

Not only did every telephone operator there get on it at once, but Saillard notified Quai des Orfèvres, where six of the duty inspectors sat down in front of phones.

'Hello? Is that the Bar des Amis? . . . Have you, since this morning, seen anything of a man, middle-aged, black overcoat, who had a boy with him of about ten?'

Lecœur again started entering crosses, not in his note-book, but in the telephone directory, which contained ten pages listing bars all with more or less fanciful names. Some were closed. In others, music could be heard in the background.

On a map which had been spread out on the table streets were marked with a blue pencil as new information came in. It was behind Place Clichy, in an alley of sorts with an unsavoury reputation, that the first cross was inscribed in red.

'There was someone like that in here around midday. He drank three shots of calvados and ordered white wine for the youngster. The boy didn't want it. But he drank it in the end and ate a couple of hard-boiled eggs.'

By the look on his face, anyone would have thought that Olivier Lecœur had just heard the voice of his son.

'Do you happen to know where they went?'

'Towards Batignolles . . . The guy was pretty drunk . . .'

The boy's father would have liked to man a phone too, but none was free, and he went from one to the other with a frown on his face.

'Hello? . . . The Zanzi Bar? Have you seen, since this morning . . .?'

Each time it was the same drill, and when one voice had finished speaking it was replaced at the other end of the line by another.

Rue Damrémont. At Montmartre's highest point. One thirty. The man's movements were becoming clumsy; he had broken a wine glass. The boy had looked as if he was about to go out to the urinal. The man had started following him, whereupon the kid had abandoned the idea, as though he was scared.

'He was behaving oddly. He kept sniggering to himself as if he was enjoying some private joke.'

'Hear that, Olivier? Bott was still there an hour and forty minutes ago . . .'

At this juncture, André Lecœur was afraid of saying what he really thought. The battle was now coming to a climax. Once Loubet had started drinking, he wouldn't stop. Was this the boy's chance?

Up to a point, yes, as long as he had enough patience to bide his time and not make any ill-advised move.

But if he put a foot wrong, if he thought the man was drunker than he really was, if . . .

André Lecœur looked up, and his glance fell on his brother. He suddenly had a vision of how Olivier might have turned out if, by some miracle, his asthma had not prevented him taking to drink.

'Yes? . . . What was that? . . . Boulevard Ney?'

They were now getting close to the city limit. This suggested that the former sergeant was nowhere near as drunk as he seemed. He was going his own sweet way, gradually, almost imperceptibly, leading the boy out of Paris itself and into the no man's land of the suburbs.

Three police vans were already on their way to the area. All available cycle-mounted officers were being sent there. Janvier jumped into the station's small car, and it was only with the greatest difficulty that the boy's father was prevented from going with him.

'But I keep telling you that you'll hear any news first by staying here . . .'

No one had time to make coffee. They were all caught up in a state of high tension which grew to a pitch where they were exchanging curt comments in clipped voices.

'Hello? Is that the Orient Bar? . . . Hello? . . . Who is this? . . .'

These words were spoken by André Lecœur. He stood up, headphones clamped over his ears, and started making strange signs with both hands. He was almost jumping up and down.

'What? . . . Don't hold the mouthpiece so close! . . .'

Then the others heard the sound of a high-pitched voice, like a woman's voice, saying:

'Whoever this is, tell the police . . . Hello? . . . Tell the police that I've got him . . . The murderer . . . Hello? . . . What? . . . Uncle André? . . .'

The voice dropped a notch and became panicky:

'I told you I'll shoot . . . Uncle André! . . .'

Lecœur never discovered who took over his headphones: he had already made a dash for the stairs. He almost broke down the door of the telegraphy office.

'Quick! . . . Orient Bar, Porte de Clichy . . . Every available man! . . .'

He didn't wait for the call to go out, leaped down the stairs four at a time and came to a stop at the door of the main office, stunned to see everyone inside completely motionless and seemingly relaxed.

In their midst, Saillard was holding the receiver from

which issued a voice that spoke in an oily, grating Paris accent:

'All right, all right! . . . Keep your hair on! . . . I smashed a bottle over his head . . . He got what was coming to him . . . I don't know what he had against the kid but . . . What? . . . You want to talk to him? . . . Come here, kid . . . Gimme your shooter . . . I don't like them gismos much . . . Well blow me! It ain't loaded . . .'

Then this other voice:

'Is that you, Uncle André?'

The inspector, holding the receiver in his hand, looked around, but it wasn't to André Lecœur that he handed it, but to Olivier.

'Uncle André? . . . I got him! . . . I got the murderer! . . . I got the rew—'

'Hello, Bott!'

'What?'

'Hello. Bott! It's . . .'

'What are you doing there, Dad?'

'Nothing . . . Waiting . . . I . . .'

'I'm glad I got him! . . . Wait a minute . . . Some policemen on bikes are coming in . . . They want to talk to me . . . A car's just stopping outside . . .'

A din of confused sounds, voices all talking together, the clink of glasses. Olivier Lecœur held the phone clumsily in one hand while he stared, perhaps unseeingly, at the map on the wall. It was all happening a long way away, near the top, well to the north of the city, a vast windswept plain where many roads meet.

'I'm going with them . . .'

Another voice:

'Is that you, chief? It's Janvier.'

By the way Olivier Lecœur held the phone out into empty space, anyone would have thought that it was he who had been hit on the head with a bottle.

'Chief, he's blind drunk. When the kid heard the phone ring, he took his chance: he managed to get the revolver out of Loubet's pocket and leaped clear. The bar owner, a tough customer, stepped in without hesitation and laid him out with a bottle . . .'

A bulb lit up on the wall map. It was the station at Clignancourt.

Reaching his hand over his colleague's shoulder, André Lecœur inserted the jack into a hole.

'Hello? Has your van been called out?'

'Someone's just smashed the glass of the emergency police phone on Place Clignancourt to report some trouble in a bar . . . Hello? Want me to call you back?'

This time there was no need.

Nor was there any need to enter a small cross in that little notebook.

Meanwhile a small boy, beaming with pride, was riding across Paris in a police car.

The Little Restaurant near Place des Ternes

A Christmas Story for Grown-Ups

The clock in its black case, which regular customers had always known to stand in the same place, over the rack where the serviettes were kept, showed four minutes to nine. The advertising calendar behind the head of the woman sitting at the till, Madame Bouchet, showed that it was the twenty-fourth day of December.

Outside, a fine rain was falling. Inside, it was warm. A pot-bellied stove, like the ones there used to be in railway stations, sat in the very centre of the room. Its black chimney pipe rose through empty space before disappearing into a wall.

Madame Bouchet's lips moved as she counted the banknotes. The bar's owner stood patiently by, watching her, while in his hand he was already holding the grey linen bag into which he put the contents of the till every evening.

Albert, the waiter, glanced up at the clock, drifted over to them and with a wink motioned towards a bottle which stood apart from the others on the counter. The landlord in turn looked at the time, gave a shrug and nodded his assent.

'Just because they're the last ones here, there's no reason, why we shouldn't give them a drink like the others,' he muttered under his breath as he walked off with the tray.

He had a habit of talking to himself while he was working.

The landlord's car stood waiting by the kerb outside. He lived some distance away, at Joinville, where he had had a villa built for him. His wife had previously worked the tills in cafés. He had been a waiter. He still had painful feet from those days, as all waiters in bars and restaurants do, and wore special shoes. The back of his car was filled with attractively wrapped parcels which he was taking home for the Christmas Eve festivities.

Madame Bouchet would get the bus to Rue Coulaincourt, where she would be spending Christmas with her daughter, whose husband worked as a clerk at the town hall.

Albert had two young kids, and their toys had been hidden for several days on top of the tall linen cupboard.

He began with the man, putting a small glass on the table, which he then filled with Armagnac.

'It's on the house,' he said.

He made his way past several empty tables to the corner where Jeanne – Long Tall Jeanne – had just lit a cigarette, carefully positioned himself between her and the till and muttered:

'Drink up quick so I can pour you another! Compliments of the landlord!'

Finally, he got to the last table in the row. A young woman was taking her lipstick out of her handbag as she looked at herself in a small hand mirror.

'With the compliments of the house . . .'

She looked up at him in surprise.

'It's the custom here at Christmas.'

'Thank you.'

He would gladly have poured her a second glass too, but he did not know her well enough. Besides she was sitting too near the till.

All done! He tipped the landlord another wink by way of asking him if it was at last time for him to go outside and pull down the shutters. It was already stretching hospitality to have stayed open this late just for three customers. At this point in the evening in most of the restaurants in Paris, staff would be scurrying around setting out tables for the late-night Christmas Eve supper trade. But this was a small restaurant which offered a regular clientele modestly priced menus, a quiet place to eat just off Place des Ternes in the least frequented part of the Faubourg Saint-Honoré.

Few people had eaten there that evening. More or less everyone had family or friends to go to. The last ones left were these two women and a man, and the waiter was not bold enough to show them the door. But the fact that they went on sitting at their tables, from which the cloths had been removed, surely meant that they had no one waiting for them.

He lowered the left-hand shutter, then the right, came back in, wavered over lowering the shutter over the door, which would force the reluctant customers to crouch down to get out. But it was now nine o'clock. The takings had been counted. Madame Bouchet had put on her black hat, her coat and her tippet of marten fur and was looking for her gloves. The landlord, his feet turned outwards, advanced a few steps. Long Tall Jeanne was still smoking her cigarette, and the young woman had clumsily caked her mouth with lipstick. The restaurant was about close. It was time. It was past the time. The landlord was about to say, as politely as he could, the time-honoured words:

'Ladies and gentlemen . . .'

But before he could pronounce one syllable, there was a single, crisp sound, and the only male customer, his eyes suddenly wide open as if he'd been taken completely by surprise, swayed before toppling sideways on the bench seat that ran along the wall.

He had walked in casually, without saying a word, without warning anybody that just as they were about to close he would put a bullet in his head.

'It would be best if you waited here for a few moments,' the landlord told the two women. 'There's a policeman on duty on the corner of the street. Albert has gone to get him.'

Long Tall Jeanne had stood up to get a look at the dead man and, pausing by the stove, she lit another cigarette. The young woman in her corner sucked her handkerchief and, although it was hot there, was shaking all over.

The policeman came in. His cape glistened with rain and gave off a barrack-room smell.

'Do you know him?'

'He's been eating here every day for years. He's Russian.'

'Are you sure he's dead? If he is, we'd better wait for the inspector. I've phoned through to him.'

They did not have long to wait. The police station was close by, in Rue de l'Étoile. The inspector wore an overcoat which was either badly cut or had shrunk in the rain, and a hat that had faded to no particular colour. He did not seem in a good mood.

'The first of tonight's crop!' he muttered as he bent over. 'He's early. Usually it comes on them around midnight, when everybody else is having most fun.'

He straightened up, holding a wallet in his hand. He opened it and from it took a thick, green identity card.

'Alexis Borine, fifty-six years old, born in Vilna.'

He recited the words in an undertone, as a priest says mass and the way Albert talked to himself.

'Hôtel de Bordeaux, Rue Brey . . . Engineer . . . Was he an engineer?' he asked the landlord.

'He might have been, a long time ago, but ever since he's been coming here he's been working as an extra in films. I recognized him several times up on the screen.'

'Any witnesses?' asked the inspector as he turned round.

'There's me, my cashier, the waiter and the two ladies there. If you'd like to take their names first . . .'

The inspector found himself face to face with Jeanne, who really was tall, half a head taller than him.

'Fancy seeing you here. Papers.'

She handed him her card. He wrote down:

'Jeanne Chartrain. Age: twenty-eight. Profession, none . . . Oh come on! No profession? . . .'

'It's what they put me down as at the town hall.'

'Have you got the other card?'

She nodded.

'Up to date, is it?'

'Still as charmless as ever, I see,' she said with a smile.

'What about you?'

The question was directed at the badly made-up young woman, who stammered:

'I haven't got my identity card on me. My name is Martine Cornu. I am nineteen and I was born at Yport . . .'

The tall woman gave a start and looked at her more closely. Yport was very near where she came from, not more than five kilometres away. And there were lots of people in the area by the name of Cornu. The people who ran Yport's largest café, overlooking the beach, were called Cornu.

'Address?' growled Inspector Lognon, who was known locally as 'Inspector Hard-Done-By'.

'I live in an apartment building in Rue Brey. Number 17.'

'You will probably be called for questioning at the station one of these days. And now you can go.'

He was waiting for the municipal ambulance. Madame Bouchet asked:

'Can I go too?'

'If you want.'

Then, as she left, he called Long Tall Jeanne back as she was making her way to the door.

'You didn't happen to know him?'

'I turned a trick with him ages ago, maybe six months . . . At least six months, because it was at the start of summer . . . He was the sort of client who goes with girls to talk more than for any other reason, who asks you questions and thinks you're a sad case . . . Since then he's never said hello, though whenever he comes in here he always gives me a little nod.'

The young woman left. Jeanne followed her out, keeping very close behind her. She was wearing a cheap fur coat which was far too short for her. She had always worn clothes which were too short. Everyone told her so, but she persisted without knowing why, and the effect was to make her look even taller.

'Home' for her was fifty metres further along on the right, in the total darkness of Square du Roule, where there were only artists' studios and single-storey maisonettes. She had a small first-floor apartment with a private staircase and a door opening directly on to the street to which she had the key.

She had promised herself she would go straight home that evening. She never stayed out on Christmas Eve. She had hardly any make-up on and was wearing very ordinary clothes. So much so that she had been shocked in the restaurant to see the young woman piling on the lipstick.

She took a few steps into the cul de sac perched on her high heels, which she could hear clacking on the cobbles. Then she realized that her spirits had drooped because of the Russian: she felt she needed to walk in light and fill her ears with noise. So she turned and headed towards Place des Ternes,where the broad, brilliantly illuminated swathe that runs down from the Arc de Triomphe comes to an end. The cinemas, the theatres, the restaurants were all lit up. In the windows, printed pennants advertised the prices and menus of Christmas Eve suppers and on every door could be read the word 'Full'.

The streets were almost unrecognizable, for there was hardly anyone about.

The young woman was now walking ten metres ahead of her, looking like someone who is not sure which way to go. She kept stopping in front of a shop window or at a street corner, uncertain whether to cross, standing and staring at the photographs hanging on the walls of the warm foyer of a cinema.

'Anybody would think she's the one touting for custom!'

When he saw the Russian, Lognon had muttered:

'The first of tonight's crop . . . He's early.'

Maybe he'd done it there rather than in the street, because it would have been an even more miserable end outside, or alone in his furnished room. In the restaurant, it had been quiet and peaceful, almost a family atmosphere. There a man could feel he was surrounded by familiar faces. It was warm. He'd even been offered a drink on the house!

She gave a shrug. She had nothing else to do. She too halted outside shop windows and looked at the photos while the luminous neon signs turned her red and green and violet, and all the time she was aware of the young woman who was still walking just ahead of her.

Who knows, perhaps she had come across her when she was a little girl. There were ten years between them. When she'd worked for the Fisheries at Fécamp – she was already as tall but very skinny – many a Sunday she had gone out with boys to dances at Yport. Sometimes she had gone dancing at the Café Cornu, and the owner's children were always running around the place.

'Don't trip over the tadpoles,' she would tell her partners.

She called the kids tadpoles. Her own brothers and sisters were tadpoles too. She'd had six or seven of them back then, but there wouldn't be as many left there now.

It was strange to think that this girl was probably one of the tadpoles from the Café Cornu!

Above the shops all along the avenue were apartments, and nearly all of their windows were lit up. She gazed up at them, raising her head to the refreshing drizzle, sometimes catching a glimpse of shadows moving behind the curtains, and she wondered:

'What are they doing?'

Most likely they would be reading the newspaper or decorating the Christmas tree as they waited for midnight. In some cases, the lady of the house would soon be receiving guests and was now worrying about whether the dinner would turn out right.

Thousands of children were sleeping, or pretending to be asleep. And almost all the people who had flocked to the cinemas and theatres had booked tables in restaurants for their Christmas Eve supper or reserved their seats in church for midnight mass.

For you had to book your seat in churches too. Otherwise perhaps the girl might have gone there?

All the people she passed either were in groups, already in high spirits, or were couples clinging to each other more tightly, it seemed, than on ordinary days.

Lone pedestrians were also in more of a hurry than on normal days. They gave the impression that they were on their way somewhere, that they had people waiting for them.

Was that why the Russian had put a bullet in his head? And also why Inspector Hard-Done-By had said that there would be more to follow?

It was the day that did it, of course it was! The girl in front of her had halted on the corner of Rue Brey. The third tenement along was a hotel, and there were others too, discreet establishments where rooms could be taken for short periods. Actually it was there that Jeanne had gone with her first ever customer. The Russian had been living until today in the hotel next door, very probably on the very top floor, because only the poorest rooms were let by the month or the week.

What was the Cornu girl looking at? Fat Émilie? Now there was a tart without either shame or religion. She was there, even though it was Christmas, and she couldn't even bother to walk a few steps up and down so that she wouldn't look quite so obvious.

She stayed put in the doorway, with the words 'Furnished Rooms' emblazoned just above her purple hat. But there she was, old, well past forty, enormously fat now, and her feet, which over time had become as sensitive as those of the owner of the restaurant, were almost terminally tired of ferrying all that flab around.

'Evening, Jeanne!' she sang out across the street.

Jeanne did not answer. Why was she following the girl? For no particular reason. Probably because she didn't have anything else to do and was afraid of going home.

But the Cornu girl did not know where she was going

either. She had turned into Rue Brey automatically and was mincing along unhurriedly, tightly buttoned up in her blue two-piece suit, which was far too thin for the time of year.

She was a pretty girl. A touch chubby. With a diverting little rear end which she wiggled as she walked. In the restaurant, seen from the side, the way her full, high breasts had pushed out the front of her jacket had been very noticeable.

'If any man comes on to you tonight, dearie,' thought Jeanne, 'it'll be your own stupid fault!'

Especially that evening, because respectable men, the ones with family, friends or just social acquaintances, weren't out wandering the streets.

But the little fool did not know that. Did she even know what Fat Émilie was doing standing outside the entrance of the hotel? From time to time, as she walked past a bar, she would stand on tiptoe and look inside.

Ah! She was going into one. Albert had done her no favours by giving her that drink. At the beginning, it had been the same with Jeanne too. Unfortunately for her, if she'd had one drink, she'd have to have another. And when she'd had three, she no longer knew what she was doing. It wasn't like that any more, not by a long chalk! Nowadays she could certainly put it away before she'd had enough!

The bar was called Chez Fred. It had a long, mahogany counter and the kind of high stools on which women cannot perch without showing a lot of leg. It was virtually empty. Just one man at the back, a musician or maybe a dancer, already in a dinner jacket, who would shortly be going to work in some night-spot nearby. He was eating a sandwich and drinking beer.

Martine Cornu hoisted herself on to a stool by the door, against the wall. Jeanne went in and sat down a little further along.

'Armagnac,' she ordered, since that was what she had begun drinking.

The girl looked at the rows of bottles which, lit from above, formed a rainbow of subtle colours.

'A Benedictine . . .' she said.

The barman turned the knob of a radio, and sickly-sweet music filled the bar.

Why didn't Jeanne just walk up to her and ask her straight out if she really was a Cornu from Yport? There were Cornus in Fécamp too, cousins, but they were butchers in Rue du Havre.

The musician – or dancer – at the back of the bar had already noticed Martine and was languidly giving her the eye.

'Got any cigarettes?' the girl asked the barman.

She wasn't used to smoking, as was patently obvious from the way she opened the packet and blinked as she released the smoke.

It was ten o'clock. Another two hours and it would be midnight. Everyone would kiss and hug. In every house, the radio would blare out verses of 'O Holy Night', and everybody would join in.

Really, it was all very silly. Jeanne, who never had problems speaking to anybody, felt quite incapable of approaching this girl who hailed from her part of the world and whom she had probably met when she was just a child.

But it wouldn't have been unpleasant. She'd have said:

'Seeing as how you're all alone and looking sorry for yourself, why don't we spend a quiet Christmas Eve together?'

She knew exactly how to mind her manners. She wouldn't talk to her about men or about being on the game. There must be a whole lot of people they both knew at Fécamp and Yport whom they could talk about. And why shouldn't she take her home with her?

Her place was very neat, very tidy. She had lived for long enough in rented rooms to know what it meant to have a place of her own. She could take the girl there without feeling any sense of shame, because she never brought men home with her. Other girls did. For Long Tall Jeanne, it was a matter of principle. And few apartments were as trim and spotless as hers. She even kept felt undersoles behind the front door which she used like skates on rainy days so as not to dirty the wooden floor, which she kept highly polished, like an ice-rink.

They would buy a couple of bottles, something good but not too strong. There were *charcutiers* still open which sold different kinds of pâté, lobster scallops and assorted tasty and attractively presented dishes which they could not afford to eat every day of the week.

She watched her out of the corner of her eye. Perhaps eventually she would have spoken to her if the door hadn't opened at that moment and two men hadn't come in, the kind Jeanne disliked, the sort of men who, when they enter a room, always look around as if they owned the place.

'Evening, Fred!' said the shorter of the two, who was also fatter.

They had already taken stock of the bar. An uninterested glance at the musician sitting at the back, and a closer look at Jeanne who, now that she was sitting down, did not seem as tall as she did standing up – which, incidentally, was why she often worked out of bars.

Of course, they knew at a glance exactly what she was. On the other hand they stared insistently at Martine then sat very close to her.

'Do you mind?'

She shrank back against the wall, still holding her cigarette as clumsily as before.

'What are you having, Willy?'

'The usual.'

'The usual, Fred.'

They were the type of men who often have foreign accents and are heard talking about horse-racing or discussing cars. They were also the sort who knew how to choose the right moment to give a woman the glad eye, walk her into a corner of the room and whisper sweet nothings into her ear. And wherever they happen to be they always need to make a phone call.

The barman started mixing them a complicated drink while they watched him closely.

'Hasn't the baron been in?'

'He said he wanted one of you to call him. He's gone to see Francis.'

The taller of the pair went into the phone booth. The other moved closer to Martine.

'That stuff's no good for the stomach,' he said, clicking the catch of a gold cigarette case.

She looked at him in surprise. Jeanne wanted to call out to her:

'Don't answer!'

Because the moment she started talking to him it would be difficult to shake him off.

'What's no good for the stomach?'

She was behaving like the dumb cluck that she was. She even forced herself to smile, probably because she had been taught to smile when talking to people, or maybe because she really believed it made her look like something off the cover of a magazine.

'That stuff you're drinking.'

'But it's Benedictine!'

She really was from Fécamp, way out in the sticks! She honestly thought that saying the name was the last word on the subject.

'Of course it is! There's nothing like it for upsetting the insides! Fred!'

'Yes, sir.'

'Bring us another here, for the lady, and make it snappy.'

'Coming up.'

'But . . .' she tried to protest.

'Just a drink between friends, no need to be scared! It's Christmas Eve, isn't it, yes or no?'

The tall one straightened his tie in the mirror as he stepped out of the phone booth. He cottoned on quickly.

'Do you live around here?'

'Not far.'

'Barman!' call Jeanne, 'give me one of the same.'

'Armagnac?'

'No. One of whatever it was you just poured.'

'A sidecar?'

'Go on, then.'

She felt furious, for no good reason, and wanted to say:

'Listen, darling, it won't be long now before you pass out . . . These guys play dirty . . . If you wanted a drink, couldn't you have chosen a more suitable bar? Or gone home and got drunk there?'

Of course she herself hadn't gone home either, even though she was used to living alone. But does anybody want to go home on Christmas Eve knowing there is no one waiting there and with the prospect of lying in bed listening to the sound of music and happy voices coming through the wall?

Soon the doors of cinemas and theatres would open and out would spill impatient crowds who would rush away to the tens of thousands of tables they had reserved in the most modern restaurants in the most far-flung parts of town. Christmas Eve junketings to suit all pockets!

Except – and this was the point – you couldn't reserve a table for one. Not least because it wouldn't be fair on folk who go out to have a good time with friends, not fair at all for you to sit by yourself in a corner and watch the goings-on. What would that make you? A wet blanket! You would see them form into huddles and whisper to each other, wondering if they should ask you to join them because they felt sorry for you.

Nor could you go out and roam around the streets, because if you did, every cop on the beat would eye you suspiciously, curious to see if you intended to use some dark corner to do what the Russian had done, or if, despite the cold, one of them was going to have to jump into the Seine and fish you out.

'What do you think of it?'

'It's not very strong.'

If her parents really ran a bistro, she should have known about such things. But it was what women always say. It's as if they're always expecting to be given liquid fire in a glass. But when it turns out to be not as strong as they'd thought, they stop being so suspicious.

'Work in a shop, do you?'

'No . . .'

'Typist? . . .'

'Yes.'

'Been in Paris long?'

He had teeth like a film star's and a moustache made of two commas.

'Do you like dancing?'

'Sometimes.'

Oh, they were laying it on very thick! How pleasant the thought of exchanging idle chat like this in such company! Maybe the girl believed they really were men of the world? The gold case held out to her and the Egyptian cigarettes too probably dazzled her eyes, as did the large diamond ring worn by the man closest to her.

'Fill us up again, Fred.'

'Not for me, thanks. Anyway, it's time I . . .'

'Time you? . . .'

'I'm sorry?'

'It's time you . . . did what? You can't be going home to bed at half past ten on Christmas Eve! . . .'

It was weird! Sitting on the sidelines and watching a scene like this being acted out always makes it look so utterly stupid. But to be involved, to play a part in it . . .

'What a birdbrain!' Jeanne muttered as she smoked one cigarette after another without taking her eyes off the trio.

Naturally, Martine did not dare to admit that, yes, she was, actually, intending to go home to bed.

'Have you got a date?'

'Don't be so nosy.'

'Got a boyfriend?'

'What's it to you?'

'Well, I'd be more than happy to keep him waiting for a bit.'

'Why?'

Long Tall Jeanne could have recited the whole script for them. She knew it by heart. She had also caught the look aimed at the barman which meant:

'Keep it coming!'

But in her present condition, the erstwhile tadpole from Yport could have been plied with the stiffest of cocktails and she would have found them not strong at all. Likewise her lipstick: didn't she have enough on already? Yet she still felt the need for more, to open her handbag and show she used Houbigant lipstick, but also to demonstrate her pout, because all women believe they are irresistible when they push out their lips to receive that impudent little implement.

'Think you're gorgeous? If you could only see yourself in a mirror, you'd soon realize which of the two of us looks most like a tart!'

But not quite, because the difference is not just a matter of a little more or less warpaint. The proof of this was provided by the two men who, as they came in, had needed only a quick look to pigeonhole Jeanne.

'Ever been to the Monico?'

'No. What is it?'

'Hear that, Albert? She's never been to the Monico!'

'Don't make me laugh!'

'But you do like dancing? Now look, sweetheart . . .'

Jeanne was expecting the word, but later rather than sooner. The man wasn't wasting any time. His leg was already pressed tight against one of the girl's in such a way that she could not draw it back, for she was too close to the wall.

'It's one of the most amazing night-spots in Paris. Regulars only. Bob Alisson and his jazz band. Never heard of Bob Alisson either?'

'I don't go out much.'

The two men exchanged winks. Obvious where this was leading. A few minutes from now, the small fat one would remember that he had an urgent appointment so that he could leave the field clear for his friend.

'Not so fast, you creeps!' Jeanne murmured, her mind made up.

She herself had also downed three drinks one after the

other, not counting the free ones she'd had courtesy of the landlord of the restaurant. She was not drunk, she never was, not completely, but she was beginning to attach great importance to certain notions.

For example, the idea that this silly kid came from the same place as she did, that she was a tadpole. Then she thought of fat Émilie standing in the doorway of the hotel. It was in that very hotel, though not on a Christmas Eve, that she had gone upstairs with a man for the first time.

'Could you give me a light?'

She had slid off her stool and, with a cigarette dangling between her lips, now joined the smaller of the two men.

He was also aware what this meant and was not best pleased. He gave her a critical once-over. Standing upright, he must have been a good head shorter than her, and the way she carried herself was mannish.

'Like to buy a girl a drink?'

'If you insist . . . Fred!'

'Coming up.'

While this was going on, the kid eyed her with a feeling close to indignation, as if an attempt was being made to steal something that belonged to her.

'Hey, you three don't look like you're having much fun!'

And, laying one hand on the shoulder of the man next to her, Jeanne started belting out the words of the song the radio was playing softly in the background.

'Of all the bird-brained . . .' she kept saying to herself every ten minutes. 'How can anyone be so . . .?'

But, oddest of all, the birdbrain in question continued looking at her with an expression of the utmost contempt.

But one of Willy's arms had now entirely disappeared behind Martine's back, and the hand wearing the diamond ring lay heavily on the front of her blouse.

She now lay slumped – literally – on the red plush seat against the wall of the Monico, and there was now no need to put her glass in her hand because more often than not she herself kept clamouring for it and gulped down the champagne greedily.

Each time she drained her glass, she burst into a fit of convulsive laughter and then clung even more tightly to the man she was with.

It was not yet midnight. Most of the tables were unoccupied. Sometimes the two of them had the dance floor to themselves. Willy kept his nose buried in the short hair at the back of his partner's head and ran his lips over the pimply skin of the nape of her neck.

'You in a bad mood or something?' Jeanne asked the other man.

'Why?'

'Because you didn't win first prize. Think I'm too tall?'

'A bit . . .'

'It doesn't show lying down.'

It was a crack she had made thousands of times. It was almost a chat-up line and just as vapid as the sweet nothings the two others were whispering to each other – but at least she wasn't soft-soaping him because she was enjoying it.

'Do you reckon Christmas Eve is fun?'

'Not especially.'

'Do you think anyone really enjoys it?'

'I suppose some people must . . .'

'Earlier on, in the restaurant where I had dinner, this man shot himself in a corner, without making a fuss, looking like he was sorry for disturbing us and making a mess on the floor.'

'Haven't you got anything more cheerful to say?'

'All right, order another bottle. I'm thirsty.'

It was the only option remaining. Get the tadpole blind drunk, because she was stubbornly refusing to realize what was happening. Make her sick to her stomach, so sick that she puked, then all she'd be fit for was to be packed off home and put to bed.

'Cheers, sweetie, and likewise to all the Cornus of Yport town and district!'

'You're from there?'

'From Fécamp. There was a time when I used to go dancing in Yport every Sunday.'

'Cut it out!' snapped Willy. 'We've not come here to listen to your life stories . . .'

When they'd been in the bar in Rue Brey, it had seemed on the cards that one more glass would have finished the tadpole off. But instead the opposite had happened.

Perhaps being out in the fresh air for a few minutes had been enough to revive her? Maybe it was the champagne? The more she drank the wider awake she became. But she was no longer the same young girl she had been in the restaurant. Willy was now slotting cigarettes ready-lit between her lips, and she was drinking out of his glass. It was sickening to see. And that hand of his never stopped pawing her blouse and skirt!

Not much longer now until everyone would be hugging and kissing and that repulsive man would clamp his lips on the mouth of the girl, who would be stupid enough to faint away in his arms.

'That's what we're all like at her age! They should ban Christmas altogether . . .'

And all the other public holidays too! . . . But now it was Long Tall Jeanne who wasn't thinking straight.

'What say we go on to some other place?'

Maybe this time the fresh air would have the opposite effect, and Martine would finally pass out. And if she did, most likely the two-bit gigolo wouldn't try to take her home and go up to her room!

'We're fine here . . .'

Meanwhile, Martine, still glaring suspiciously at Jeanne, talked about her in a whisper to her beau. She was probably saying:

'Why is she interfering? Who is she? She looks like a . . .'

Suddenly the sound of jazz stopped. For a few seconds, there was silence. People rose to their feet.

The band struck up 'O Holy Night'.

Oh yes, it was here too! And Martine found herself squeezed tightly to Willy's chest, their bodies melded into one from feet to foreheads and their mouths scandalously stuck together.

'Hey, you disgusting pair! . . .'

Long Tall Jeanne bore down on them, shrill and

loud-mouthed, arms and legs moving jerkily like a puppet with its strings crossed.

'Aren't you going to give anyone else a look in?'

And then raising her voice:

'Shift yourself, girl, and make a bit of room for me!'

When they didn't move, she grabbed Martine by the shoulder and yanked her back.

'You still haven't got it, have you, you stupid cow! Maybe you think your precious Willy here has got eyes only for you? But what if I got jealous?'

People at other tables were listening and watching.

'I haven't said anything up to now. I didn't interfere, because I'm a decent sort of girl. But that punter is mine . . .'

Startled, the girl said: 'What's she saying?'

Willy tried to push her away but failed.

'What am I saying? What am I saying? I'm saying you're a rotten little tart and that you stole him off of me! I'm saying you're not going to get away with it and that I'm going to smash your pretty face in. I'm saying . . . Take that for starters! . . . And that! . . . And this! . . .'

She went at it with a will, punching, scratching, grabbing handfuls of hair, while onlookers tried in vain to separate them.

Long Tall Jeanne was as strong as a man.

'You've been treating me like dirt! You were asking for it! . . .'

Martine did her best to fight her off, scratching back, even sinking her small teeth into the hand of her opponent, who had her by one ear.

'Calm down, ladies! . . . Gentlemen, please! . . .'

But Jeanne kept screeching at the top of her voice and managed to knock the table over. Glasses and bottles shattered. Women customers fled from the battle zone screaming while Jeanne finally succeeded in tripping the girl and putting her on the floor.

'Ah! You've been asking for trouble and you've come to the right place for it! . . .'

They were now both on the floor, grappling with each other, spattered with flecks of blood from cuts caused by the broken glass.

The band was playing 'O Holy Night' as loudly as possible to cover the noise. Some of the customers went on singing. Eventually the door opened. Two officers from the cycle-mounted police patrol marched in and headed for the fighting women.

Unceremoniously they nudged them with the toes of their boots.

'Come on you two! On your feet!'

'It was that bitch who . . .'

'Shut up! You can explain down at the station . . .'

As chance would have it, the two men, Willy and his pal, seemed to have vanished.

'Come along with us.'

'But . . .' Martine protested.

'Keep your mouth shut! Save it for later!'

Long Tall Jeanne turned to look for her hat, which she had lost in the scuffle. Outside on the pavement, she called to the doorman:

'Jean, keep my hat safe for me. I'll come and get it tomorrow. It's almost new!'

'If you don't keep quiet . . .' said one of the policemen jangling his handcuffs.

'Aw, put a sock in it, dumbo. We'll be as good as gold!'

Martine's legs gave way. It was only now, all of a sudden, that she started to feel sick. They had to stop in a dark recess to let her empty her stomach against a wall on which was written in white letters: 'No Urinating'.

She was crying, a mixture of sobs and hiccups.

'I don't know what's got into her. We were having such a nice time . . .'

'Come off it!'

'I'd like a glass of water.'

'You'll get one at the station.'

It wasn't far to the police station in Rue de l'Étoile. It turned out that Lognon, the hard-done-by inspector, was still on duty. A pair of glasses was perched on his nose. He was busy, probably writing up his report about the death of the Russian. He recognized Jeanne, then the girl. He looked at each of them in turn, not understanding.

'You two knew each other?'

'Looks like it, sunshine.'

'You're drunk!' he barked at Jeanne. 'What about the friend? . . .'

One of the policemen explained:

'They were both rolling on the floor of the Monico, tearing each other's hair out . . .'

'Inspector . . .' Martine started to protest.

'That's enough! Lock 'em up till the van comes on its round.'

The men were on one side, not many, mostly old

down-and-outs, and the women on the other, at the far end, separated from them by a wire grill.

There were benches along the walls. A pint-size flower-seller was crying.

'What are you here for?'

'They found cocaine in my posies. It wasn't nothing to do with me . . .'

'You don't say!'

'Who's she?'

'A tadpole.'

'A what?'

'A tadpole. Don't try to work it out. Careful! She's going to throw up again. That'll make it smell like roses in here if the paddy-wagon's late!'

By three in the morning, there were a good hundred of them in the lockup at police HQ on Quai de l'Horloge, men still on one side and women on the other.

In thousands of houses, people were still probably dancing around Christmas trees. Digestive systems were certain to be struggling with turkey, foie gras and black pudding. The restaurants and bars would not close until it started to get light.

'Have you got the message at last, you silly cow?'

Martine was curled up on a bench as highly polished by use as any church pew. She was still feeling sick. Her features were drawn, her eyes unfocused, and her lips pursed.

'I don't know what I ever did to you.'

'You didn't do anything, girl.'

'You're a common . . .'

'Shush! Don't say that word in this place! Because there are several dozen of them here who might skin you alive.'

'I hate you!'

'You could be right. Even so, maybe you wouldn't be feeling so clever at this moment if you were in some hotel room in Rue Brey!'

The girl was clearly trying to make a big effort to understand.

'Don't bother trying to work it out! Just believe me when I say you're better off here even if it isn't comfortable and don't smell so good. Come eight o'clock, the inspector will give you a short lecture that you thoroughly deserve and then you can get the Métro back to Place des Ternes. Me? They'll give me the usual medical and take my card off me so I can't work for a week.'

'I don't understand.'

'Oh forget it! Did you really think that spending the night with that creep – and on Christmas Eve too – would have been nice? Did you? And how proud of your precious Willy you'd have been tomorrow morning! Do you really think people didn't feel disgusted when they saw you hanging round the neck of that cheap crook? But now at least your future is still in your hands. And you have the Russian to thank for it, you know!'

'Why?'

'I dunno exactly. Just a thought. First because it was on his account that I didn't go straight home. Then again maybe it was him who made me want to be Father Christmas for once in my life. Now move up and make room for me . . .'

Then she added, already more than drowsy:

'Just imagine if, once in their lives, everybody behaved like Father Christmas . . .'

Her voice grew softer the deeper as she drifted into sleep.

'Just imagine it, right? . . . Just once . . . And when you think of how many people there are on this earth . . .'

Then finally, still muttering, with her head on Martine's thigh for a pillow:

'Can't you stop your legs jumping all the time . . .'